After
Happy End

Rita Kinsky

To my dear, dear friend Donnachka with love.

Rita Kin

ISBN: 1453737707
ISBN-13: 9781453737705
Second Edition

DEDICATION

To my grandma

∾

TABLE OF CONTENTS

PREFACE

This book is about love, dignity, drugs (and what they do to you and everybody around you), self-responsibility, and values.

All events and characters are complete fiction, but the message I am trying to convey is real.

If there are any people who can relate to my story and at least one person who can find answers, it will have been a worthwhile effort.

I hope you laugh with me and cry with me.

ACKNOWLEDGMENTS

Two public figures inspired me to write this book.
I hope this book will be worthy of my
disclosing their names someday.

NOTES

Things my grandma had said or could have said

Don't compare your situation to someone who is doing better; compare it to someone who is doing worse.

Don't worry before and after; only worry after.

It is better to help somebody than have to be helped.

Don't accept any favors; you will have to pay for it dearly later on.

Don't compromise on anything important; you will have to pay for it dearly later on.

You can only enjoy something if you earned it.

If everybody cleans his or her own house before volunteering to help others, no one will need help. (The sick and orphaned are excluded.)

Don't try to please everybody; it will attract all the wrong people. You need only a few people around you who share your values.

If you fail to teach your child to fish to feed him or her for a lifetime, you cannot expect others to give your child a fish to feed him or her for a day.

There are two categories of people in the world: those who can open someone's briefcase or someone's letter, even just to look in it, and those who cannot do it for the world.

Money is an indicator of everything. If a person is not kosher as far as money is concerned, you don't want him or her as a friend.

Don't show off; the poor will be jealous, and the rich will be laughing.

You must save money for a rainy-day fund. The rainy day will inevitably come, and when it comes, you have no right to other people's rainy-day funds. (The sick and orphaned are excluded.)

Never lie and your life will become much simpler.

Don't live by emotions; live by reason.

Honey, you are reading so many books not because you are so smart but because you are so lazy.

Remember, you are not just getting a horse—you are getting a whole stable (referring to the families when Greg and I were getting married).

It is noble to help your neighbors pay for their funerals; it is a disgrace not to save money for your funeral so that your neighbors have to pay for it. (The sick and orphaned are excluded.)

❧

AFTER THE
HAPPY END

PROLOGUE
GLIMPSE INTO THE PAST

I stood at the intersection of two busy thoroughfares waiting to help my son, Danny, cross the street after school. Holding the case with his violin, I watched as he ran in my direction, waving at me and screaming with delight. Not that he was looking forward to his violin classes, but he was very happy to see his mom, brag about another A he had gotten that day, and eat our usual danish pastry. Twice a week, I ran to this spot during my lunch break to walk him to his music school and switch his backpack for the violin. I would go to work with the violin in its case in the morning and leave work with the backpack in the evening. My coworkers were always making fun of me—I was a crazy mother. Nothing was more important in life than what Danny ate, how Danny felt, and what grades Danny brought home to his mama. I always had a fresh danish for this occasion; he hungrily ate it while we hustled to the music school a third of a mile away. I teased him that danishes were named after Danny because he liked them so much. His music teacher demanded that I stay during the class so that I knew what he had to do when practicing at home. Danny was a very promising little violinist. He was a very promising anything; he was so gifted, my little prince.

My marriage was less than stellar, so my life revolved around work, friends, and of course, Danny. We were inseparable.

My husband had a life of his own—although he adored Danny, too—so I also had a life of my own. With my work, my friends, my books, and my Danny always by me, I was content. I could see that men liked me. Very deep inside, I maintained traces of hope that, one day, someone may truly love me—maybe in my next life.

If anybody had told me many years ago, when we still lived in the Soviet Union, where life would take me, both literally and figuratively, I never would have believed it. Do you ever have random memories of some unimportant moment that just sit in your brain for no reason? This was one of them.

Here is another flashback: I am sitting in a huge music hall, where my little gorgeous seven-year-old Danny is standing on stage, wearing a black tuxedo, and playing a violin concerto accompanied by an orchestra. Never in my life did I experience such euphoria. People around me, mostly other parents, were so amazed by his performance that they started asking each other whose boy it was. I can still feel that state of complete happiness, that feeling of fulfillment.

And then that not very happy, but nevertheless stable, life ended one day when somebody called me at work to tell me that my husband was in love with another woman. I have a vivid image of myself standing at my supervisor's desk holding the phone and feeling numb. It is another moment that flashes through my mind sometimes. I wish I had forgotten that one. Oh well, it all happened in the last life and even the last century.

Today, I am a world away from all that.

∽

PART I

NEW BEGINNING

CHAPTER 1
HELLO

So let me introduce myself. I am Victoria Kolman. My friends call me Vika. I am a Russian American, but I prefer to call myself just an American. I came here years ago, yet I am still in the honeymoon phase with this country, as I have a much less appealing place to compare it to. It is like marriage—only by having a bad husband first can you appreciate any other normal husband. But we will talk about that some other time.

So, I am in love with this country, which makes me sound very primitive and naive nowadays. Well, all my life, I was part of the Russian intelligentsia, which means you have to be sarcastic about everything in the world. But I changed my ways, and you will have to excuse me for being such a simpleton and becoming a patriot of this country.

I cannot clearly state what the main reason was for my emigration from Russia. First, my beloved brother and his family left Russia to live in America, and I missed them dreadfully. Second, my very intelligent son grew up hating everything in that system, and I knew he would have ended up in jail should we remain there. He was, indeed, a political refugee. And, third, my husband fell deeply in love with a younger girl. Since he was never a womanizer, it was clearly a very serious relationship, and I just could not take it anymore—all that collective agony. When my husband finally decided he would have to leave this girl behind and come to the States with our son, Danny, and me, we left Russia and came here.

Thus, I cannot claim any true heroic motive; we just had to leave. Danny was the initiator of our flight from Russia and begged me not to give his father a hard time as long as he agreed to come with us; otherwise, we all had to stay. Danny promised we would always be inseparable, he and I, just the way we always were.

I expected to go through horrible nostalgia, depression, and withdrawal and was pleasantly surprised that I never had any. I did my best not to have time for it.

Any new beginning is hard, but mine was dreadful because my husband just couldn't get over that girl. He took out his frustration on me, and life became unbearable. When I warned him that I would leave if he didn't treat me as normal husbands treat their wives, he said, "You know I love her. But we made an agreement, you and I, and I will do my best to try to continue living with you."

"That's not good enough," I replied. "I know I can be loved. Go screw yourself. Danny and I are leaving."

Little did I know that Danny had decided to stay with his father. After I told my husband I was leaving, he invited the love of his life to move from Russia, and there they were—my husband, some stranger, and my Danny—living in the one-bedroom apartment meant for our family.

I was not prepared for such a blow. Things like that couldn't happen in real life—at least not to me.

I pleaded with Danny.

"Danny, why are you doing this to me?"

"Do you want me to do it to Dad instead? You have friends and relatives here; he has no one. He says he always took care of me when I needed him, when I was sick."

"Danny, you're fourteen years old. Don't you remember *who* always took care of you? We were always inseparable, you and I, while your dad was off living his own life?"

"I don't know. That's what he says. He wouldn't lie."

"I am sure he believes it himself to this day. He has always believed his own fantasies. Today, it just so happens to be a very convenient fantasy for him. But you must remember everything because you're an adult, Danny. I can't believe this is happening."

"Are you saying that it's my fault that all of this happening?"

"Of course not! It's our fault, not yours. But, now, when your dad's girlfriend is here, why don't you run back to me, even if just to comfort your mother? You're my whole life. Don't you know that?"

"I don't want to be your whole life. Live *your* life. I've come to a new country to start a new life, not to watch my life become terribly complicated by the two of you. I am sick and tired of you always being miserable. First, you were sad that he had a girl, and then you were sad that we couldn't leave Russia because of that. Then we finally make it here, and you're still sad because your marriage isn't working, anyway. What a surprise!"

Did he blame me for all this? Wasn't I the victim? I couldn't understand it.

He went on, "Now you're sad that I don't want to live with you. I hate both of you, but at least with him, I don't have your constant attention. I want to be left alone."

"Danny, I promise not to bother you or interfere with your life. Just come live with me. I'll rent a better apartment if you don't like this one. We'll go on vacation. I'll buy you a new computer, a new television, anything you want."

Was I losing my mind bribing him?

"No, it's easier with Dad. You bring out the worst in me. The second you open your mouth I want to argue and say nasty things. Then you start crying, and I feel bad and hate myself for doing that to a woman. I have enough problems on my plate without worrying whether I hurt you. Just leave me alone and live your life."

"Darling, let's go get some therapy. Let's analyze what has happened to us. Please, I beg you."

"You go get some therapy. I don't need any."

This is what parents don't realize when they start entertaining the idea of divorce. They don't consider that, one way or another, their children will get even with them. Had I known that would happen, would I still have left my husband anyway? Probably. But before making that decision, I would have thought long and hard about all the potential repercussions. I was stupid enough to assume that my son belonged to me. And I was too busy with my misfortunes to notice that he had grown up.

Was he just being a rebellious teenager, or had he grown up too fast and become a very angry adult at only fourteen years old? I didn't know the answer, but the fact of the matter was I had to learn how to live without my Danny.

Sometimes, when I couldn't cope with the situation, I would go see my brother, Greg. At first, he didn't understand what happened with Danny.

Then, one day, he said, "Vika, I'll tell you what I think happened: He loved you excessively when he was little—I remember it. And when he realized that you were suffering and couldn't help you, all he could do was start hating you for being unhappy. If I were your ex-husband, I would never let our son slip into hating his mother. That is so low of him; that is beneath any decent man. I don't know, Vika," he added. "We don't believe in divorce in this family. Remember Babushka Leeza?"

"I always do."

"Be tough. We'll survive."

Our grandma, we called her *bubbe*, the Yiddish word for *babushka*, which is Russian for grandma. She was a legend.

❦

CHAPTER 2
MY BUBBE

My grandma Leeza was born in the year 1900. She witnessed all the horrible and great events of the crazy twentieth century. But to say that she witnessed it is to say nothing. She *lived* that crazy twentieth century. She was born to a very poor family of eleven. All her parents worried about was how to feed their nine children. Four of the nine died very young, and only five children lived. My bubbe was a very pretty girl. I saw her picture when she was a young woman, and I can tell you that she did look very beautiful—they call it a biblical beauty. Considering her physical beauty and incredible mental strength, I can say for sure that our family did not produce anybody even close to what she was.

I wish I had listened more carefully to the tales she told us about her life, but who cared about her prehistoric stories then?

When she turned nine, her parents sent her to live with some wealthy family as a nanny. She told us it was the first time in her life when she ate more or less normally because she was allowed to finish the spoiled toddlers' leftover food.

At seventeen, she fell in love with their poor neighbor. He loved her very much in return as well. Her mother had died by that time, and her father told her that, being penniless herself, she could not afford to marry another penniless person.

Then along came my grandfather. He was from the same poor neighborhood, but he was considered a great catch because he worked at the big bread factory and was allowed to bring home some bread. He started to court my bubbe, and her father suggested that she had better welcome his attentions. She married him and regretted it all her life.

She always remembered that first guy and what could have been. Of course, she could have been unhappy with that boy, too, but at least she would have only herself to blame for making a bad choice. But if the choice is not even yours… Have you ever noticed that when you make some big mistake based on your own poor judgment, you try to learn from it and never look back? At least I do. But when you make a mistake based on someone else's suggestion, it hurts and angers you tremendously forever. At least it does me.

By the time her son, Michael, was born, they had survived the First World War, the Great Social Revolution, and my grandpa's first mistress. He had mistresses all his life. It's hard for me to be objective because it concerns my grandma, who lived for us, and my grandpa, who lived for us as well.

My grandma adored her son. She told us he was her pal, her soul, her sunshine. He hated his father and cherished his mother—at least that's what she told us. My grandpa was a very handsome, uneducated, and unintelligent person. After the revolution, all the nobility and the elite were exterminated or imprisoned, and illiterate proletarians like my grandfather took important posts. He became the head of the union committee at the factory where he worked. I remember Bubbe told us he complained to her that the politically active women who worked with him had short haircuts and wore lipstick, which turned him on, but she did not.

One day, my bubbe found a good job as a cashier at the diner for the elite communist party members and decided she could afford to kick him out. When she broke the news to him, he said he would kill himself and took a rope, went to the attic, and staged an unsuccessful hanging. When she told me this story, she was so matter of fact. She said she didn't believe he had the strength to do it and was more afraid of what the neighbors would say about all of it, as they all lived together in a big apartment. So she stopped his spectacle with the rope and told him she would give him a second chance. She made a promise to herself that she would not have more children. In a year, she found herself pregnant (with my mother) and did everything possible to get rid of it; abortions were illegal, and birth control was nonexistent. It obviously didn't work, and my mom always blamed my grandma for her weak health, claiming she was affected when in the womb. My grandma made it up to her by slaving away for her, her husband, and the rest of us—all of her life.

My bubbe had a huge family; her siblings who survived each had numerous children. During Stalin's time, part of the family disappeared, and my bubbe always took care of her nieces and nephews in need. My grandfather and my mom complained that they took advantage of her. Well, who knows?

When the Second World War reached Russia and the Germans were making their way to our city, my grandma collected her two children and her then-disabled husband and left the city on foot, taking only blankets, water, and some bread. They had to leave the blankets behind after the first night because they were too tired to carry them any longer. At one point, they met a man in the forest who was fleeing, too. He said the Germans were coming to the village they were passing; they could even hear the sound of machinery. My grandma gave her son and daughter a blade and told them to slit their wrists the moment they saw the first enemy soldier had spotted them, as she was well aware of what the fascists did to the Jews in Poland. My mother was sixteen years old then and a very spoiled child. She cried that they could do whatever they liked to her, but professed she was too young to kill herself. My grandma then told her son that he would consequently have to help his sister before he killed himself. As for her, they all knew she would not need help; she was an iron woman.

My mom always told us that if it were not for her protesting, we would not be here today. While she was fighting with her family, the Germans passed by without noticing them, and miraculously, they made it through the forest and arrived at a small train station. There were people waiting to board the train, and somebody informed them that the last freight train was supposed to pick up whomever was there. They were barely able to board the train because there were so many people there already. They stood in the overcrowded cargo car for two days, during which time German planes bombed the train a few times, and many were killed. Finally, the family made it to a small town near the Ural Mountains and decided to stop their flight and take a breather—a breather that lasted four years.

My grandma found a job at the train station's diner and rented a small room nearby, and my grandfather moved to a bigger city to work at a military plant. He visited his wife and daughter a few times during those four very long years. My mother was sent to school, and my uncle Michael contacted his medical school, which had been evacuated to another city. He went there to finish his last year, received his diploma, and became a military surgeon. He spent three years on the front lines, and my grandma prayed for him day and night.

My grandmother helped many people. When she saw families in the passing trains with sick people or children, she would take them to her place, feed and clothe them, and force the family to stay with them until they were well. She always refused to take any money, saying, "You will need it at the next station."

After the war, my grandmother, grandfather, and mother came back to our city. It was absolutely ruined. But we had won the war, their immediate family had survived, and nothing else mattered. Almost all of my grandma's brothers, sisters, nephews, nieces, and their spouses and young children—sixty-four of them—had died in the Jewish ghetto. Only a small few who were in the army had survived. My grandma took care of all of them, and later, their families, as long as she lived.

My uncle Michael stayed with the military. He was sent to Mongolia, where he started sending very disturbing letters to his mother. He was having some problems with military Special Forces, which was like the KGB, and was trying to get transferred elsewhere. Even though we had won the war, Stalin's dictatorship did not become kinder toward his own people. My uncle Michael, who had survived the Great War, disappeared from the face of the earth about a year and a half after it ended. My grandma made one inquiry after another, and finally, she received a letter saying that her son had drowned while drunkenly swimming in the river. He never drank, and he was the best swimmer in high school and college. Also, since Mongolia was a foreign country and the Soviet Union was shut by the Iron Curtain, there was no way for my grandma to go there and at least visit his grave. My grandmother kept his letters and two pictures of him her entire life and told us to bury them with her. Only when I was placing these letters in her coffin did I bother to read them. It was so awful. He knew what was coming, and neither he nor she could do anything about it. And it was obvious how much he loved her—so much love was in those letters. I couldn't see her replies to him, of course, but from the tone of his letters, I could say that hers were full of love and encouragement. I hope they were buried with him as his were with her.

My grandma had a Mason porcelain tea service her son had brought her from Germany. Only one cup and saucer survived our childhood, and I treasure it very much now. Every morning I have my coffee in this cup with the broken handle. This is all that's left of a human life, of a very brilliant and sweet person—one cup and one saucer. But they say one lives for as long as one is remembered. Grandma, uncle Michael, you are safe with me—and with my Greg, I am sure.

I know every life is a heartbreaking story, and every grandmother's story is a big, dramatic book. Plus, every person who survives any war has tons of stories like this. I would not normally bother you with all these sad things that happened so many years ago, but there is another reason I am telling you all of this.

When my grandma finally received word about her son—word that he was no more—my mother was married to that "good catch," my father, for seven months and was six months pregnant with my big brother, Gregory. My grandma did not tell anybody at home about this news, so as not to upset my pregnant mother. She went on pretending that nothing had happened until my mother gave birth. And only then did she break the news to her husband and daughter. Now, this is the reason I decided to tell the whole story—to show you how strong and incredible a human being can be and what emotional control he or she can possess.

She was the one person who had the biggest influence on the adult I became. She never kissed us, and she never baby-talked to us, but she set an example none of us could ever match. I'm not exaggerating in saying that not one day goes by without my remembering her. Sometimes, I pray to her. I believe she is still around somewhere to protect all of us, as she did when she was with us. Her personal life was joyless. She never talked to my grandpa; they just coexisted in the same apartment. She lived purely for her daughter and for us.

While growing up, I remember many of the people whom she helped during the war sent her greeting cards. One particular family from Leningrad often invited us to visit. My bubbe and I finally went there one summer, and it was a blast. And, while there, I learned something I never would have imagined could happen. Thinking it would impress me to know that my bubbe once had an admirer, one of the two sisters she saved told me they had a brother, and when my grandma visited them right after the war, he fell for my bubbe! He was a bachelor, and he fell in love with her. He even asked her to marry him!

I was outraged. I was disgusted. My old bubbe, whose sole purpose in life was to serve us, and me in particular, could be in love with somebody besides Greg or me? Yuck, she was forty-five when that happened. Forty-five is *very* old; people don't even think of such things when they are that old.

She liked him, too, but she would not be my iron bubbe if she allowed herself to be happy.

"No," she said. "In my family, people don't divorce. It's a disgrace."

She sacrificed herself for the approval of her son (who was still alive then) and daughter, all of us (her future descendants), and her relatives, friends, neighbors, and strangers. Anybody was more important than herself.

Today, being older than she was then, I know how wrong of her it was to let that opportunity pass by. She was only forty-five years old—a young and beautiful woman who knew no joy in her life!

How bleak and unkind her life was to her! She was married all her life, but she never had a husband. Her son died, and her daughter presented her with a very disrespectful son-in-law. But I never heard one complaint from her. I only regret that I did not listen when she volunteered to tell her stories or to teach us something. And I regret being a naughty little girl. I had character, you know. I still do.

∽

CHAPTER 3
MEET GREG AND NELLY

I rented an apartment around the corner from Danny so that he could at least visit me as often as possible, but he never did. I saw him a few times a year. He was just fourteen years old, and I have no right to judge him. A child is not supposed to be in situations where he has to choose between parents. It makes him confused and angry.

Every morning, I would start my car and then proceed to start screaming while driving to work. The emotional pain was unbearable. I liked the company I worked for very much. I was nearly the only woman on the whole floor. There are not as many female engineers here as in Russia. I was showered with male attention and made some very good friends, so business hours were full of hard work and nice people.

My evening ritual repeated that of the morning; I would start the car and start screaming again while driving home. I can't remember when I stopped doing this. Probably after a year or so. I was getting used to being single. I was married my entire adult life, and it took some effort for me to learn how to care only about myself. At any point during the day, I would think of Danny and try to imagine what he was doing at that moment. My Danny, who I attended to for twenty-four hours a day all my life...

My big brother, Greg, was very supportive of me—as far as a brother can be supportive of a sister. He would call to ask me if I needed any help with changing the oil or fixing the faucet. But I was craving the other kind of support. As for his wife, Nelly, she did not like the fact that I was single; according to her, it was almost embarrassing. They very seldom invited me to any gatherings except family events. When they went somewhere with their friends, I was never invited. Was she afraid that I would not pay for myself? I always did. I am very meticulous when it comes to money. I could not understand why they purposely avoided taking me anywhere with them. Nelly once said including somebody single makes the company of couples defective. She didn't think I would start flirting with her girlfriends' husbands, I am sure. And I could not understand why I should feel myself defective; I did not feel that way at all. I felt myself a whole person. I always did—thanks to grandma.

Regardless, it hurt me a lot. I knew it wasn't Greg's idea. I remember times when I would go to the beach or to a concert and run into Greg and Nelly and all our mutual friends, some of whom had known me long before they knew Nelly. They would all rush to greet me and were evidently very happy to see me, so I didn't understand why Nelly intentionally excluded me.

Only here in America did I learn that judgment and control were considered to be real sins. I never thought much of it before. But Nelly came here years before me, and she should have been aware of it. And judging and controlling she was.

I always thought complex people were sophisticated and interesting people. But there is something else to that notion. People have layers. Have you thought of it before? Neither have I. But now I literally can tell you how many layers any person has. The most solid and straightforward human beings have one layer. I know very, very few of these types of people.

It doesn't mean they are shallow, not at all. It means they have standards and always follow them no matter what. They don't need to lie or manipulate; it is easy to deal with them, and they gain your respect. And, most importantly, you know what to expect from them because they mean what they say—forget lying or beating around the bush. It doesn't mean they have to tell you inconvenient truths and always be downers. It's not what they say; it's what they do. They live by it. These people seem inflexible and primitive at first, but in the long run, they always win, and you are lucky to have them in your life.

The majority of people have numerous layers of different colors and consistencies—the one for work, the one for their friends, the one for their spouses, and always the separate one for their children. Some of their layers are crystal clear, while some are dark and ambiguous, and some even have sub-layers.

Nelly had 328 layers. And every day, sometimes every hour or minute, she consistently changed them. When I first met her, I fell in love with her sweet disposition. She was so smart and brilliant and hospitable and supportive. She would listen to you for hours and be so understanding. She really attracted people with her larger-than-life personality. It was no wonder that Greg fell head over heels in love with her even though she was not the most beautiful girl on the block. Then, in time, I noticed a pattern; she would attract you, pry into your life, and make you dependent on her liking you. And then, when you were at her mercy, she would judge you, depending on her ever-changing moods and her approval or disapproval of what you said or even what you did in your life. She would judge anybody in the world as if she were God, and you had better agree with her judgment.

I became dependent upon her alternating moods of happiness and depression. Sometimes she would be cold with me, and I felt so miserable that it made me go out of my way to please her. The days and weeks when she was in that dark mood were exhausting; she would suck the energy from you. Then, all of a sudden, she would become a loving and approving mother to you again, and you felt that your beloved Nelly was back, that she still loved you, and that you could love yourself again. You tried to forget the misery you just went through and dismissed it as a misunderstanding.

And then everything would repeat until, one day, I decided that I couldn't afford to let anybody suck so much energy out of me; I had a life and a family of my own to worry about. I told myself that I didn't care what Nelly thought of me, that I didn't have to listen to her very controlling advice, which was more like a command. And life became easier and simpler. But a consequence of that liberation was exclusion from her closest circles, and as a result, some of our dear friends, whom she still had on a very short leash, were afraid to be as close to me as before. Oh well, freedom doesn't come free. They all became collateral damage.

Lately, the days when one could see Nelly's clearest and warmest layers were rare. But when it happened, you enjoyed being with her, watching her, and remembering your happy, young days. But you also knew it would pass, and when it did, you wouldn't be hurt anymore. Three hundred and twenty-eight layers Nelly had.

CHAPTER 4
M&M

I had a very close friend at the time. Her name was Maggie, and her husband's name was Max, so I called them "M&M."

We were just acquaintances at first, but the more dramatic my life became, the more dedicated friends they became. Like back in Russia, friends sacrificed for friends. M&M didn't leave me alone for one evening—forget the weekends. When I was not at work, I was always in bed. I was so weak I couldn't move. Greg forced me to have blood drawn to make sure I didn't have mononucleosis.

M&M would call and offer to take me along to visit somebody they had befriended. I would excuse myself, attesting that I was very sick and could not get out of bed. Since I could not explain what was wrong with me, the official version was that I had a forty-eight-hour flu every weekend. But Maggie would not have it; they would come to my place and drag me with them somewhere. Every time we passed the building where Danny lived, I would grab Maggie's hand and say the same thing: "My son lives here, and I am passing by like a stranger. There is his door, and I, his mother, cannot even open it to see him." Maggie would just squeeze my hand, and after a few times, she remembered not to take that route.

Maggie and Max—they probably saved my sanity at the time.

I am still surprised I didn't kill myself. But I am probably a survivor—I am my bubbe's girl. I *forced* myself to believe that my own life was very important, too. And I *forced* myself not to think of Danny all the time.

As for my relationship with America, every year I enjoyed the feeling of freedom more and more. I didn't long for it in Russia; I didn't know what it was. I think this is the story of all totalitarian countries. Maybe they don't need freedom because they don't know what it is and how it feels. Anyway, my head still spins from the smell of freedom. Even when I lost my first job and almost lost my first place, it never crossed my mind that this "ruthless" country didn't care for a poor single woman. On the contrary, I blamed myself for not being responsible, for not saving money for a rainy day as my grandma would do, and for buying something I couldn't afford. It taught me a good lesson; it was almost my first real-life lesson on personal responsibility. Do you think I feel jealous that some stupid ladies like me are being offered bailouts nowadays? No, I am better than that. I can handle my life, and if I cannot, I had better learn how.

For a few years, I searched for my own niche in this new world because my mechanical engineering profession was not in great demand. I had always been a good scholar. I tried a lot of things, and I have so many certificates and diplomas that I could wallpaper my garage. Boy was I fighting for survival. There were no programs or welfare or whatever else for me to consider. Why? You already know the answer: Because I knew I could do better than that. I did not come to this country to be a parasite.

I am not going to put you through the list of things and events I went through. Otherwise, you would get tired of me, quit reading, and miss the real story. We have made it to the beginning of my story—good for you and good for me.

෴

CHAPTER 5
BACK TO LIFE

In my second year of screaming in the car on the way to and from work, I decided I had to put myself back on the market. As a woman who was married for so long, I felt very uncomfortable with dating. I wish to forget the succession of my potential suitors.

Suitor Number One met me at Starbucks. He was a divorced nephew of my mother's new friend, Aunty Tanya. His first question was whether I would like to have some coffee. I hesitated, but said yes. He bought the largest cup of brewed coffee they had, asked them for an extra cup for me, poured half of it into my cup, and generously invited me to add milk and sugar to my taste. His second question was what I did for a living. I answered. After only fifteen minutes, he pronounced that he liked me. His third question was how much rent I paid for my apartment. I answered.

I wondered whether he had a first-date questionnaire and if his next questions would be how much I made, how much I weighed, at what age I had my first period, and to what political party I belonged. I dreaded having to use profanity, which I prefer not to do unless really pressed, but he didn't ask any more questions. My rent amount was enough for him to make an important decision: allowing me move in with him (if we got along) to help him pay his mortgage. My current rent money would be a fine contribution, according to him, as long as I did all the cooking. But not to worry because we would share the grocery expenses—of course, provided I collected all the receipts.

He called the next night, to which I responded that I didn't go out on weeknights, only weekends, and that I didn't drink coffee so late in the day. He called again that Friday night, and I said I was coming down with something. He sounded very irritated. The hardest part was learning how to say, "Thanks but no thanks." I had never been very good at saying no to anybody about anything. Greg sometimes joked that he liked women who didn't know how to say no. Danny called me a people-pleaser. I argued with him that it's good if everybody likes you; it's good for your karma. Now I am not sure about that anymore.

My potential husband number one never called again. Aunty Tanya said I thought too much of myself and stopped talking to my mom.

Suitor Number Two called me and said that he was my mom's apartment building manager's son's friend. He asked me whether he could stop by and visit me at my place. I wasn't sure about that, but I could always call my next-door neighbor, Larisa, another single Russian woman on the market, for help. I was so lucky to have her as a neighbor. She had never tried to be too close, and she had never knocked on my door to eat Russian borscht together. I loved her for that. I had her keys to feed her cat when needed, and she had my keys to water my plants when I was out of town. My plants liked her much better than they liked me. I was always forgetting to water them, but she never forgot. We saw each other once every few weeks and both enjoyed this kind of relationship—perfect neighbors. I asked her to stay on our shared balcony for the next half hour and just pop up at my place after that.

He entered with roses and a box of chocolates. Wow, that was refreshing! He said he liked my place very much and asked whether I rented or owned. It sounded as if he wanted to run my credit report. Maybe he did—one cannot be too careful nowadays. I had just bought my condo and told him that. His chocolates suggested that we would have to have tea, so I offered it to him, and he said that he would love some. I put out the only three cups and saucers I had and—absolutely unexpectedly—Larisa opened the door.

"I'm so sorry! I just came to water the plants! Vika, why didn't you tell me that your plans had changed?" she screamed.

She was so shy she refused to join us for tea, but I insisted. My number-two suitor was very attentive; he moved chairs for us and offered to help with everything. I counted the minutes for this awkward date to be over. Then he expressed that he wanted to tell me about himself. Larisa suddenly remembered she needed to go home to take out her cat, whatever that meant. She left, and he told me the story of his life. He had been married and had a son and a daughter. He divorced his wife because they had financial disagreements. He never saw his children because he was afraid that his wife would remember to apply for alimony, which she never did for some unknown reason. Now his children were all grown up, and he wanted to renew ties with them, but they refused. He said that he even sent his daughter an expensive gold necklace for her sweet sixteen, but she never called him to thank him. His ex didn't even teach her daughter to say thanks to her own father for an expensive gift. I didn't have anything to say about any of it. It was all so foreign to me.

He left saying that he liked me a lot and that I knew how to listen and not interrupt. He said he would call me soon. He let a few days pass to make a woman get a little worried and called me that weekend. I said I was sick and suggested we shoot for the next weekend. I couldn't think of a good reason to say no. If my mother encountered complications with her manager, I would feel very bad.

When he called the next weekend, I explained that I had considered everything and concluded that he was definitely too good for me. He had lived in America for seven whole years and I for only three. He was very upset with me; he sounded so angry, as if I had broken our engagement. Then he said it was just as well and asked if I could give him Larisa's phone number. I was so relieved that I did something very unethical: I gave him her number without asking her permission.

Later that night, Larisa came to visit and asked me whether I was hurt that he called her instead of me. He told her that he liked her better from the beginning, but as a noble man, he didn't want to ask her out without leveling with me first. I assured her that I was very happy for both of them and had no hard feelings whatsoever.

They started dating, and she stopped talking to me. Later, she sold her condo when they bought a house together and got married. I lost my perfect neighbor. And I told my mother to stop giving out my phone number left and right.

"And what are you going to do? Go to a bar to pick up a husband?" she asked.

"Who told you I need a husband?"

"With a mortgage like that?"

Then so-and-so who knew so-and-so called, asked how long I had lived in America and whether I had children, and said he would call me on the weekend, but never did.

Suitor Number Six was a friend of a friend of Greg. We met at the plaza. He offered to buy a frozen yogurt for me. I declined. I was always very sensitive when it came to people spending money on me; I'd rather pay myself.

He said, "In that case—your place or my place?"

I turned around and went home.

Suitor Number Nine called me, and we started talking to each other every night. He was very sharp and very funny. Check. He loved music and so did I. Check. He would put on an old jazz record, and I would listen to it over the phone. I went out of my way to sound my best, to be as witty, as funny, and as well read as possible. We began to really develop a relationship, and it went on for a couple of weeks. Then, one night, he called to tell me that he had bought an old Glenn Miller record and put "Moonlight Serenade" on for me. Anyone who knew Glenn Miller when still in Russia was definitely a friend of mine. He said he wanted me to come to his place that night and meet him at last. I preferred to meet him in a public place the first time, but he sounded so offended at my suggestion. Plus, he was a good friend of Nelly's friend Mila's ex-husband's ex-partner. So considering the close relation to my family, I felt somewhat secure. I was so nervous; it was the first time I was getting ready for a real date with somebody I really liked since I had dated my husband. I spent a good hour making sure I looked my very best and then drove to his place, which happened to be very close to me.

We experienced a somewhat awkward moment when we first saw each other, because when befriending someone on the phone, you start imagining that person's looks, and then when you see him or her in person, you have to adjust your mental image. He looked like a fine man of my age. Check. He said he did not expect me to be *that* pretty. That felt good. Check.

He put the record on, and we talked for a half hour. Then he came to me and hugged me as if inviting me to dance. It felt quite uncomfortable, and I freed myself from this unexpected embrace. He pulled me closer and started passionately kissing me. I jumped back and breathlessly tried to explain that I was not ready, that I needed more time, and that it had to come naturally.

His face transformed into that of a madman as he ferociously grabbed my arm and began dragging me toward his bedroom. I fought vehemently to release his grasp and begged him to wait for another time and treat me in a civilized manner. But he held me firmly and threw me on his bed. I screamed that I would call the police and report a rape. I managed to jump from the bed and grab the phone. I dialed 911, but he flew to pull the cord from the wall. I threatened pressing charges against him and vowed that everybody would know he had raped me.

All of a sudden, he ran to the hall, opened the front door, and screamed, "Get out of here now!"

I ran for my life. I was such a mess that I forgot I had driven there and ran all the way home. The next morning, I walked back to get my car and prayed not to meet him.

He called two days later to apologize. He said he had lost his mind and that it would never happen again. Our relationship had looked so promising; we could have had everything if he had behaved in a normal manner. But, at that point, I didn't want to see or hear from him again, so I hung up. He called again and started to mock me and threaten me. For the next two weeks, he called me every night and talked to me very nastily. I called Nelly's friend, Mila, and warned her that I would have to call the police to report his stalking and verbal abuse if it did not stop. She apologized profusely and promised she would talk to him. The next day, his friend who had given him my number called and identified me as a whore who went to a stranger's house, had sex with him, and then bad-mouthed an honorable man, but apparently, everybody knew that I was a slut.

This was a whole new world to me after being married for fifteen years to the boy who had kissed me for the first time in my life. Welcome to a single woman's world.

He eventually stopped calling. From then on, I swore to myself that I would try to be with the first man of normal age, height, weight, profession, and looks who was not a criminal. Each of my previous suitors looked like a great catch now.

CHAPTER 6
ALEX

A few uneventful months passed when I received a call from a guy named Alex who said that he'd gotten my phone number from our mutual friends. He explained that he was very busy and that if I agreed to meet him, he could only do it three days from then, between the hours of 5:30 to 6:30, and at the particular plaza where he had to pick up his dry cleaning. Wow, what a romantic encounter. But, by that time, I had made that profound decision, so we met. He was very skinny, very angry, and not exactly my type, which was a professorial intelligentsia: a little unkempt, not too sporty, but witty and sarcastic, and usually complete with an ulcer. Alex, on the other hand, was very neat, well built, and not too sarcastic. But I promised myself to give it a chance. After spending more time with him, I realized that I liked his company and that we complemented each other well. But when we talked on the phone, it was as if he were a different person—more primitive and angry. I had already met somebody, however, who was gentle on the phone and unpleasant in person. Alex was not too good with words, but when we met, it was more and more congenial every time.

A month later, on a Sunday, we went to the beach and met my friends. They were all impressed by him and declared that he was rather handsome, which surprised me. If I were to tell you that I don't care how men look, you would never believe me. But I don't. At least I never did until then. He taught me to care. I always thought women had to be concerned with their looks, but men—who cares how they look? I know, I know, don't be upset with me. It was wrong, and I retract my previous point of view.

So he happened to be handsome, and it was a bonus. But I don't think it played a role in my deciding whether I would date him. It was not love at first sight for me or for him. I don't believe in love at first sight—not for me, anyway. I cannot love somebody for his eyes or his nose. I can love the person for his personality only. But that's just me. Perhaps other people maintain, shall we say, differing opinions...

On our first date, he said I looked a little like Yoko Ono. Something in his voice suggested that he was not particularly fond of Yoko Ono's appearance. But who did he think he was not to like how she looked if John Lennon loved it? Well, I absolutely don't agree that I look anything like her, but at least now you know how I look. Although, as I said, I don't look like her at all...

One thing struck me as positive in him: He had values. It was so unusual and refreshing. My sister-in-law, Nelly, called him "provincial," because once he became my official boyfriend, he wanted to spend all of his time with me and become acquainted with my family and the scariest thing—my son. I tried to hide this man from everybody in my life, while he paraded me around to all of his friends, acquaintances, and daughter, introducing me with "This is my Vika." Being the independent and open-minded woman, I should have hated it, but I liked it—a lot. It was so unusual for me to be considered and important to my companion.

His character was slightly rough. Also, he was not the most generous man who ever existed. But he was the first man in my life who honestly thought I was very important and was not shy in showing that to me and to everybody he knew. And he listened. He paid attention to everything I said. That was refreshing, too. He was very considerate of my wishes and would never force anything on me. And, later, he proved to be a very considerate man in bed as well.

Sometimes, we went out for a walk or to dinner and returned to my place. He would stay there very late, but always went home to sleep. We both treasured our space.

One Sunday morning, some six months after meeting, we were walking on the beach, and Alex suddenly said, "I don't know where this is going, Vika. First, I thought that I wanted something very serious. But the more serious our relationship becomes, the more doubts I am having. I have been giving it a lot of thought. All I want in life is to take it easy. I have had my share of distress. You are the type of woman who a man has to marry. It's not right to continue to just date you. I really like you a lot, and it scares me because I don't think I want to get married again."

The way he put it was so insulting, so blunt. I had not asked him to marry me. The thought had not even crossed my mind yet. Why would I jump into that again after seeing somebody for just a few months? I was not a kid. He didn't even ask me whether I *would* marry him. It was offensive in every way. It was too offensive whether I said, "No problem, I want to keep dating and just have a companion," or "No, I don't want to see you anymore if you don't want to marry me." He was so stupid; he couldn't even find a normal way to explain himself. He didn't leave me any choice. We had to break up. I asked him to drive me home, and we said good-bye.

I made a decision. No more dating for me. Period.

I had forced myself to emotionally detach from him. It was not easy, but necessary.

A month later, the people who introduced me to Alex invited me to attend their younger daughter's sweet-sixteen party.

They assured me Alex wouldn't be there, so I said I would definitely come, as they were very dear friends. When my friend opened the door, she apologized that Alex had called at the last minute and said he would come, too. She explained that there was nothing they could do. Apparently, he had also expressed his desire to talk to me. He was a very difficult person. Instead of calling me, although I would not talk to him, he had to come and make everybody feel uneasy. I told my friend that she didn't have to worry; I could look after myself. She had the party to take care of. I had barely crossed the threshold into the house when I immediately spotted Alex, who came right over to greet me. He was very inflexible and bold as usual.

"Vika, I really miss you. Of all of the women I've dated here [he was more stupid than I remembered], you are the one I don't want to let go. I want to continue with what we had together and possibly even get married one day." He clearly thought he was making me feel better.

"Alex, you forgot to ask me whether I would even consider marrying you."

"Why wouldn't you? I'm not too hard on the eyes, and other women have liked me before you. Plus, I'm hardworking, and when I'm with a woman, I know only one woman—the one I am with."

"Until the next one comes your way?" I added jokingly. I wanted to turn this conversation into small talk.

"So what do you say to my proposal?"

"I say nothing. Let me go inside and greet the birthday girl."

I went inside, gave the little precious her birthday gift, and left.

When I got home that night, he called and said, "Vika, this is the last time I'm offering you my affection, my companionship, and my help. If you say no now, you will never hear from me again."

"Alex, you never said that you had any feelings for me."

"We're adults. I want to give it a serious try. Isn't that a good enough reason for you? You know that I am not very good with words."

"I think you *are* very good with words if you want to hurt somebody."

"Yes or no?"

"I need to think about it. I finally got you out of my system, which took a lot of effort. Now I have to decide whether I want to let you back in."

"Can you decide by tomorrow night? I will ask you one last time."

The next night, when I returned home from work, the phone was ringing as I opened the door.

"Vika, have you decided? Do you have anything to say to me yet? I want to see you. I miss you so much it hurts. Do you call it feelings? Why do you need to make me suffer?" He sounded angry.

"Alex, *I* made *you* suffer?"

"Do you want me to apologize? I was honest with you and said what I thought. I never play games. If you want me to apologize for it, I will apologize."

"And what do *you* want, Alex? Do you think I can just forget that conversation?"

"How much more time do you need? I will call you the same time tomorrow. It will be the last time I ask."

This was the third time he had said that. I considered calling his bluff, then thought better of it.

In twenty-four hours to the minute he called.

"Good evening, Vika. Yes or no?"

I knew I couldn't play games with him, even to teach him a lesson—that is, if I wanted him back.

"Maybe," I responded in an attempt to save face.

He started laughing with relief. "I will see you tomorrow," he said.

The next day, Maggie invited me to her mother's birthday party at their tiny apartment after work. I adored her parents, who were very simple, very warm people, not as sophisticated as my father, but so much better and kinder. They were my family when my parents were still in Russia and my husband and son disappeared from my life. I told Alex we were both invited, which wasn't necessarily true, but M&M were easy.

Maggie opened the door, saw us together, and said to Alex, "Are you back in the picture again? I would not take you back so easily if I were her."

Alex knew Maggie already, and they got along just fine before. They would be just fine again, I was sure. We all sat around their small round kitchen table, and it felt so good. I felt at home with these dear people around and with Alex next to me. Alex took my hand in his under the table, and an electric shock shot through my entire body; I had never experienced anything like that. Perhaps some chemistry existed between us after all, but can chemistry create an electric current? I would have to ask Danny—he's big on science. When Alex was pressed to say something, his voice was very low and hoarse. I think he was feeling the same sensation.

On the way home, Alex had his left hand on the wheel and his right hand on my hand. We did not utter a word until he parked. My head was spinning, and I felt dizzy.

"Vika, I will stay tonight."

"Yes."

It was the first time he stayed through the night. Our love flourished. We could not get enough of each other. He learned to talk. In fact, he turned out to be a very good conversation-alist when he was happy and not under pressure. Once he referred something or somebody (like a woman or a place or a car) as his, it became the best in his opinion. I learned that about him later. So now he commented that my oriental eyes looked bigger, that I was prettier than he had thought me to be before, and that I cooked as good as his late mother—and that was some compliment.

CHAPTER 7
GETTING TO KNOW EACH OTHER

I met Alex at a time when I was still working but knew a pink slip was imminent. Three months after this last development, I finally lost my job. I had no money to pay the mortgage exactly two months after my last paycheck. I was receiving unemployment and moving heaven and earth to land another job. Danny was in college and working full time, and I had to help him no matter what it took for me.

I don't know whether Alex was deeply in love with me by then or was just being an honorable man, but he offered to move in with me to help pay the mortgage. That's how we started living together—not too romantic.

He was an engineer back in Russia, as we all were. Being a Jew in Russia meant you could only attend the polytechnic college. Once he arrived in the States, however, he didn't care what his occupation was as long as he could provide for himself and his daughter. So he became an electrician, and a good electrician at that. Being an electronics engineer previously helped. I learned another lesson from him: Prestige is worth nothing. A highly professional person is a respectable person by definition. He took pride in what he was doing, and I loved to look at his big, beautiful, scratched hands when he came home and ate dinner. His hands were gentle, strong, and powerful. When I had a headache, he put his hands on my head, and in a few minutes, the pain was gone. He was a brilliant student while in school, and his dream was to become a doctor. He tried getting accepted into medical school for years, but of course, he had no chance for the same reason that we could only go to polytechnic colleges. He did have very special hands; he would have made a brilliant surgeon. Oh well, in that country and in that system, they didn't need you to fulfill your talents. The government and the collective decided what you would become and what you wouldn't become.

It is interesting that he, unlike most of us, always hated it there. In our family, words like *capitalism*, *America*, and *dollars* were prohibited. My parents were pure products of the Soviet system.

Maybe it is time to introduce my parents to you before we go any further.

CHAPTER 8
MY PARENTS

I told you already that I am a representative of the Russian intelligentsia. And the reason why is that my parents are also members of the Russian intelligentsia. So that's how we were brought up—cynical, nihilistic, obsessed with books, criticizing the system, but despising those who openly stood against it. We were very comfortable. We knew our limits in society and enjoyed not worrying about trying to do better. Our attitude was quite slack: "Whatever, we are bigger than any system anyway." We all had many friends in Russia, and we actually lived for them. We gathered together in the evenings and on the weekends to talk, to discuss the latest literary publications, and to be sarcastic in general. Sense of humor was our god. Any kind and non-cynical person was considered a fool.

We did care about clothes and other material items, but since we had no means to acquire it, the women in our circles knitted, sewed, and altered whatever we could obtain. (*Obtain* was a very popular word. "I obtained very cool shoes, but they are three sizes too big, and I actually need a coat more. Want to switch?" That actually could be a real conversation.)

If you needed to move, to carry a piano to the fifth floor with no elevator, or required help of any other kind, your friends were always there for you. And you were always there for them. That was how we survived, and we liked it.

My parents were typical products of the system. My mother was a doctor. Although she made very little money, she had enough connections to obtain some chicken or even deli meats for holidays a few times a year. She was very proud of her resources, especially when she managed to get a beef or pork tongue, which was her specialty. Oh, my mother's tongue…

My father was an educated cynic. He couldn't succeed in his career as far as position or money went, so he and my mother created a niche for him. He was declared an "unrecognized genius," an official term in our household. I never asked my maternal grandmother whether she accepted that title for him, and now we will never know what she thought of it. My mother took as many night shifts at the hospital as she could to make some money. My grandmother came in the morning to see us off to school, and then she would cook, clean, and do the laundry until it was time for her to leave, precisely twenty minutes before our dictator came home from work.

My brother and I competed for his approval. But when he was not pleased with us…oh my God, he need only glance at us with that special look of his, and we were mortified. His motto was "I am always right, even when I am wrong." He was famous for his sense of humor. But it worked only one way. He would joke about anything, hurting people just for the sake of a joke. And if somebody became offended, he and my mother would rationalize, "He or she doesn't understand jokes." But God forbid somebody should make a joke about him. He would reply so sternly that people would remember not to make the same mistake again. We called him "Himself," and it was the one joke he approved and tolerated.

My mother often mentioned that my father could easily get a PhD to make more money like some of his friends. I never asked in what field he could become a PhD. But it didn't matter. What she was really saying was he could get a PhD as easy as that if he only wanted to or if this imperfect world could recognize such brilliance.

My mother created a monster, and we had to deal with it. Other than that, our childhood was very happy, as happy as any when you look at it from a distance many years later. We especially enjoyed when our grandma rented a cottage in the village, and we lived there for the whole summer every year, leaving our parents behind. Those are the brightest memories I have from my entire childhood. That's where we grew up, and if there is anything right or wrong with me, blame it on that godforsaken place.

When my parents were dragged to America by the mere fact that both of their children moved to America, my mother adjusted immediately and became as active and business-oriented as usual. It was a drag that she didn't have to use connections to obtain those precious delicacies; beef tongue was available at any supermarket, so it lost its charm.

As for my father, he hated everything here. "Material things are not important," he said. So what if they got a subsidized apartment in the city center? "The ceilings are never as high as they were in our apartment [one bedroom for the two families] in Russia," he said. So what if they received a pension on which they could live very comfortably? "There are some things one cannot buy with money," he said.

"A person is supposed to die where the person was born," he would declare.

"Says who?" I would ask.

"Says I."

Then it hit me that the reason he denied America was America's refusal to recognize him as an unrecognized genius. There was no audience to be sarcastic and brilliant for any longer. People were recognized by their ability to be valuable and to support themselves, to make money and to be self-sufficient, and this was wrong to him! They also dared not speak Russian in America. His children, and especially his grandchildren, became more educated than Himself. They spoke that "evil language," according to him. He started a crusade against American education and culture in general.

He complained about everything. Not even the weather was right in Southern California. Yes, it is the best climate in the world, but you cannot deny that some days in December are not as pleasant as some days in August. Also, a week or two in July can be too hot. Yes, we don't have humidity here, but that is also bad because we become humidity intolerant. Thus, when a few days a year happen to be humid, we feel we are suffocating. America is generous to the old people among immigrants and gives them necessary and unnecessary things—but why shouldn't she?

The goal of his old age became proving to his family (Who else would listen?) that no one was more brilliant or more important than he. Even when he spoke of his children and grandchildren to his old friends he would belittle them.

"How is your family?" his friends would ask.

"Do you really want to know?"

"Why, yes. How are Greg, Vika, and the kids?"

"They are very busy making money. That's all they care about—so materialistic. They go to college, and they learn to make money. They make money to buy houses and to send their children to the best colleges so that they, too, can learn to make money. Take my grandson: He is so practical that he knows how to get a job, how to get a loan, how to remodel his house with his own hands, and how to change the oil in his car. I remember myself at his age—what a romantic dreamer I was! We were getting together with friends, drinking and smoking all night long and talking about important things, about soul. I knew nothing about making money—it was beneath me. If not for my mother-in-law, we would have starved. That's what

I call being a real intellectual. People are getting smaller, don't you think? Especially here, in this pragmatic country."

That's my father's philosophy now. This country is for those unsophisticated, materialistic creatures that actually produce things so that the crème de la crème of intellectuals can sit back and be sarcastic about it.

CHAPTER 9
THE FAMILY MEETS ALEX

I took Alex to my brother's house to introduce him to my family and friends.

When we sat down at the dinner table, Greg asked him, "What would you like to drink?"

"I don't drink," Alex replied.

Silence followed, and I knew that was the wrong answer. He sensed it, too.

"I'm sorry, but my father was an alcoholic. He made our lives miserable. He also loved meat and fat women. So I don't drink, don't eat meat, and like skinny women," he added, which didn't help the situation at all.

I got the impression that my friends and family didn't like him too much at first glance, or should I say, at first word. He did not strike them as a cool and funny guy. Oh well, he didn't initially strike me as one, either. But, as I said, he had values that were so rare that, for once, I didn't care about my brother's opinion—something that had never happened before. Except for Greg, all of the men in my life—my father, my ex-husband, and my son—treated me with so much sarcasm that I enjoyed being taken seriously for a change.

Nelly called me that night—another seldom occurrence. She usually had Greg call to pass along her message to me. But, this time, she called to share her happiness for me that I was now like all of them and not the one poor relative who always came alone. She declared that I could go everywhere now and be treated as all respectable women. And that's after being married for fifteen years and raising a teenage son. But it wasn't news to me that Nelly made the rules in life—or at least she thought so.

But forget Nelly. Back to my new, exciting life. For the first time in my life, I could talk to a man, and he would listen and pay attention and understand. We could talk for hours; I couldn't get enough of it! When I talked, he listened, because everything I said was important to him. He didn't have too many friends—not as many as I did, anyway. He said again and again that I was his only true friend and that all other people were purely acquaintances. Nelly referred to him as "provincial" again. If being a somewhat undedicated friend to hundreds of people, but an extremely dedicated husband is provincial, then I'll take provincial any day. My ex-husband was an outstanding friend to others, but a lousy husband. So I knew which one I preferred.

When we went out, he was careful not to make me jealous. He was a handsome guy, and women would throw daring glances at him. He was five years my senior, yet he didn't look his age. I could envision how it was when he was single. But he was so afraid it would make me mad that he only looked at a pretty girl with an approving eye when I was looking the other way. It was funny. Provincial is always provincial.

He also continually complimented me when we went out. He would say that I was the prettiest woman in the room, which was a big stretch, of course, but it felt good nonetheless. He liked me more by then—as long as I stayed skinny. He started to drink a little more so as to not be considered the black sheep between our friends and family. He still didn't eat meat. And he still admired skinny women.

We had another test to pass—meeting with Danny. Danny and the other four boys had rented a house not too far from the college. We couldn't afford the exorbitantly priced dorms, as we couldn't afford to pay for the on-campus parking, even though Greg had given him his old Toyota Corolla. This car had a very interesting feature: You could only start it if you buckled the passenger's seatbelt first, whether you had a passenger or not, and then turned ignition. Was it my little pampered Danny? He worked and went to college, getting around by bike, yet he still managed to be a very good student. When my Danny set his mind to something, he meant business. He had come to this country to succeed.

He allowed me to visit him every third Sunday.

One particular Sunday, I gathered all my strength and decided to take Alex with me to introduce him to Danny. I cooked a full trunk of food, as I usually did, and we drove to his house. The first five minutes or so was awkward, but then we settled in and became more comfortable. I furtively stocked his fridge with all the food I had prepared, so as not to aggravate him. He would force me to take it back if I did it publicly. But I knew by now that if I left it there, he would eat it later.

I offered to treat both Danny and Alex to lunch at any restaurant of Danny's choice. It's usually easier to alleviate tension when out at a restaurant, where the atmosphere and meal provide good distractions. Danny and Alex were getting along just fine. I marveled at the sight of my Danny eating nonstop. I ordered a ton of food, as if for myself, and when it arrived, Danny ate it all while talking to Alex. Alex tried to make Danny feel comfortable and relaxed by asking him many short questions, which Danny responded to with long answers. Quietly sitting there as a bystander to the conversation, I learned some news. I also realized Alex, should he and I stay together, could be my ambassador to the world of Danny, who held men in a higher regard than women. Was it a Russian thing, or was it related to his issues with me? I didn't know. But Alex had become handy in a new way.

That night, as we were leaving, Danny said, "I can't believe my mother remembers how to smile. Maybe we can all get together more often—like every other Sunday?"

CHAPTER 10

JULIA

Julia is Alex's daughter. Her main characteristic is her beauty. It is her destiny, her occupation, her birthright, and her ticket to self-indulgence as well as other's indulgence.

When we first met, Alex simply stated, "I have a daughter, and I adore her. She is very pretty." That summed it up in a nutshell. Looks were the most important thing to both of them. When we met various mutual friends, he would make statements like, "Wow, he doesn't look well at all. Did you see his stomach?" It drove me crazy. I would quickly retort, "Not to mention that he is a vice president of a major company and both his sons attend Ivy League schools."

Julia married at sixteen, during her first year in America, to an older and richer guy. He treated her nicely, and as long as she could shop till she dropped on Rodeo Drive, she was in love with him, too. She visited us a few times after Alex moved in with me, and she talked to me kindly, but condescendingly, as if she were some superior creature. She was into top designers, while I was unemployed at the time. Even if I were working, I would never in my life spend such money on clothes or drive anything so ostentatious, anyway. She liked to turn heads. I did not. I thought it was bad for my karma. Not that I was a head-turner, so I was safe there.

By the time I met Alex, she had been married to that guy for a few years. It was obvious she hailed from a different world. But what did it matter to me if she gallivanted around in a parallel universe? What mattered was that Alex was from my universe—or so I thought.

CHAPTER 11
THE HAPPY END

The first year Alex and I lived together was not too easy; we both had to substantial adjustments. But we were both determined to make it work, and we put forth the effort to succeed. We had many important things in common, and that was what really mattered.

One day, we went to visit an old friend of mine. Her husband had passed away, and she had been living with her boyfriend for a few years. He didn't want to get married, and she worried that after five years, or however long it took to be considered a common-law marriage, he could claim her house and leave her.

After returning home, Alex insisted that he didn't want things like that to stand between us and offered for us to get married. Believe it or not, that was how he proposed. I had hoped it would be more romantic, but by that time, I knew him well enough to understand that he is not a talker, but a doer. So we went to Las Vegas and got married. We always joked that we got married "drive-thru" style and nevertheless lived happily ever after. Alex bought me a delicate wedding band and promised to buy my engagement ring later, when we could afford a better one.

When we returned from Las Vegas, I was hopeful that somebody would throw a surprise party for us. This second marriage, as a second chance, was a big deal and a big commitment for me. But, evidently, neither my family nor my friends thought too much of my becoming Victoria Lansky. I had to talk Maggie into agreeing to pretend that she was throwing the surprise party for us, although I was behind everything—buying the cake and alcohol, booking the restaurant, and sending the invitations from her. I invited about ten or twelve people; it was not a huge affair.

When we arrived at the place and Alex saw everybody, he was so upset that he left the room and almost left the restaurant. I ran after him.

"We got married. Let's start living a married life—as simple as that," he pleaded. "Why do we need all this? I hate attention! We both had our big white weddings already, didn't we? And it didn't work out very well, did it?"

Being an honorable man, he returned five minutes later and said, "Well, we're here already. I will not let you down. It's not your fault, and therefore, I cannot embarrass you. Let's go and celebrate. I just need to drink a little more today."

That's my Alex.

That's the Happy End.

PART 2

AFTER THE HAPPY END

CHAPTER 12
FIRST THREE YEARS

We could not afford a honeymoon right away, so we decided to postpone it to sometime in the future, when we would make it even more memorable. In the meantime, we enjoyed our honeymoon at home and went ahead with our everyday lives as before, working and doing chores. We looked forward to living our happy and quiet life together. We wanted it quiet because we both had our share of thunderstorms in the past. But it was different now: We both liked being married. We became even more important to each other.

I already knew Alex was a good family man and would make a good husband, but even things like opening a joint account and saving money together felt like luxurious and sexy things. We hadn't been spoiled in our previous marriages, so we could really appreciate and enjoy the little things other couples took for granted.

Every time we left home, he would say, "Have I told you lately?" It was his cute way of saying I love you. Every night when he returned home from work, the first thing he did was kiss me. He did it automatically, and it felt *so* good. I was practically a pampered little wifey. When he drove and I sat to the right of him in the passenger seat, he would put his right hand on my shoulder, and my heart would melt. And on the weekends, with his hand on my shoulder as we drove home after spending the day at the beach, I would repeatedly gush, "I love my life."

Another thing we valued above all else was intimacy. Again, only when you lose something do you really appreciate it when you find it again. We treasured what we had. Alex was a very tender man. When he put his gentle, yet powerful hands on my shoulders and kissed my lips and then my neck, the earth moved under my feet, and the outside world did not exist anymore.

I also noticed that Alex always agreed with my opinions about other people and always comforted me when I thought I was wrong in regard to a given situation. He definitely applied a double standard when it came to me, and it felt good. Because I was his wife now, he vowed to always be on my side whether I was right or wrong. But this implied that I had to do the same, and I decided to attempt to learn how to do it. I hate double standards, and I think they are unacceptable regardless of the circumstances—be it family, friends, or politics. But I decided that, for love, one could make an exception.

He taught me one other thing: Do what you think is right and don't worry about what other people will say. He helped me break free from the constant worry about other people's opinions, which had enslaved me my whole life. What a feeling it was!

Every night we held hands while falling asleep. It felt as if I were reviving and recharging before facing the next day. I could physically feel it. Remember the ceiling of the Sistine Chapel by Michelangelo and those famous hands that almost touch? God touches Adam's hand, and life begins. Force those hands apart, and life ends. That's how I felt: Force our hands apart, and our beautiful world we created ends.

I was on good terms with Julia by then. Although we had different priorities in life, she was a very sweet and friendly girl, and she was open to cultivating a relationship, as was I. She obviously wanted her father to be happy, so there was not a hint of jealousy. When she called, we could talk for hours about life and anything else; she would listen to anything I said. When she visited us, she routinely asked for a book to read. I would give her something I considered essential, but it had to be about love, of course. She was ignorant, but smart and eager to learn. I bemoaned her neglectful mother and carless upbringing as well as her choice in husband, who didn't have anything to offer her except money. She had everything to become a bright and intelligent young woman, but her beauty was probably enough for her mother, her father, her husband, and herself. I was so naive at that point of my life I imagined that I could become a surrogate mother to her and that we would have a whole life ahead of us to develop a mother-daughter bond. Alex marveled at this prospect.

Six months into our married life, Julia called and said she wanted to discuss something with me. She didn't want to live with her husband anymore. I was sure it had to do with her intentions to go to college, become somebody, and live a more meaningful life. I reminded her that it was entirely her decision, but I would support her if she decided to do it. And I promised to talk to her father. When I told Alex what we were discussing, he was outraged.

"I absolutely forbid her to do it until she gives me a good reason. I always worried about her and was very relived when she got married to a normal, caring guy."

"Alex, it is her life, and she has to decide."

"Vika, I also forbid you to fill her mind with ridiculous ideas. I know you would like her to work, go to college, and become a scientist or an opera singer. She would do those things without you if she were made for it. Her husband is just what she needs. Where do you think she will live when she leaves him?"

"She will stay with us for a couple of weeks until she finds an apartment and a job. This is America. She won't be the first young girl who works, lives with roommates to pay the rent, and goes to college. That's how Danny lives."

"I'm not sure she's capable of that. Did she tell you this is what she plans to do, or are these your fantasies?"

He called her and yelled at her—an exceedingly rare occurrence.

"I forbid you to leave him. You constantly praise him for everything! What could be wrong with him now? Did he get physical with you?"

"Of course not, Papa. What are you talking about?"

"Then promise me that you will not do anything stupid without talking to me."

"Nothing will happen, don't worry. I changed my mind."

Julia didn't bring up this subject anymore, and then a month later, she moved to our place with two suitcases full of her best clothes—just like that.

When we started questioning her, she simply replied, "He's no fun anymore."

Later, we learned she had started an affair with a younger man, who, of course, was one of the reasons. That young man disappeared from her life very soon as well, and a chain of new friends started showing up at our place. She would sleep during the daytime and begin getting ready for her nightly escapades

60

in the evening, when we were about to go to bed. I could not start arguing with her yet because we had become friends just a few months ago. Coming from an entirely different world, I was very uneasy and apprehensive about her lifestyle. I couldn't believe that respectful and reasonable Julia could all of a sudden transform into this wild creature. I urged Alex to restrain her and compel her to obey the rules of the house where she had so unwittingly decided to belong. He was hurt by my comments.

"Vika, were you not young once, too?"

"Alex, are you suggesting that you think this is how I lived my life when I was young? Did you?" *Alex, I thought, with all his very strong values…*I continued, "You do a disservice to your children by applying double standards to them. You have to see them realistically."

He shot back, "Vika, maybe this is why your son hates you."

It was the first time he hurt me like that.

The plan was for Julia to find a job and start saving money to rent a place of her own. She started working as a front-desk clerk at some medical office. Every morning, I would try to wake her up so that she went to work. For the first two weeks I was almost always successful. She would leave for work, and I would go to my job late every morning. But I refused to let her stay behind; I knew she would never get up on her own.

Every evening, she would take a shower, do her hair, dress up, go out, and return in the wee hours of the morning. The problem, however, was that we had only one shower in our one-bedroom condo, and it was located in our master bedroom. I was normally in bed and asleep by the time she came to our shower to get ready for some nightclub. As a matter of fact, she could enter our bedroom anytime she wanted.

When I complained to Alex, and he complained to her, she would scream, "Is it my fault that you guys have only one shower? What do you mean I don't have to blow-dry my hair when Vika is asleep? I am going out with my friends, and I must do my hair. Don't you get it?"

When she went shopping and came home with bags and bags of clothes, she would explain to us, "This is my way of dealing with distress. I am going through a divorce, and you have to be supportive."

"Julia, why did you buy those white boots? You have ten pairs of boots already," I would dare to ask.

"Don't you see that I must have white ones because I bought that beautiful white cashmere coat last week?"

"It's very harmful to your health to go out every night and then go to work every morning." Alex would try to change the subject, so as to not irritate her too much.

"If I were living a life like you two, like two worms, I would kill myself," she replied.

Sometimes her friends came to visit her, and they spent time on the balcony smoking and laughing. I had a new neighbor who shared my balcony after my old neighbor, Larisa, moved out. One day, she came to us complaining that she could smell marijuana smoke wafting in from the porch and threatened to report us to the police if it happened again. I was outraged. How dare she insinuate such things?

I asked, "How do you know it's marijuana? The kids are smoking cigarettes."

She said, "Don't tell me you cannot tell cigarettes from pot."

The truth was I could not. I knew nothing about any of that. I was so humiliated by her visit that I cried.

Alex was upset with me for overreacting. "This is not a big deal. All children go through a marijuana stage. Were you not young and stupid yourself?"

"Alex, you yourself never even drink beer. Don't give me this baloney!"

"All right, all right, I will talk to her. No more smoking pot at our place."

When confronted, she lectured us, "You have to stand up for yourself! No one has the right to tell you what to do! No one has the right to tell *me* what to smoke! I am a grown woman. I was even married. Everybody smokes pot! It's your property! That bitch! I hate her!"

But her friends stopped coming to our place.

She had moved in with us for what was supposed to be a few weeks. Six months later, nothing indicated that she was seriously thinking of saving money and renting an apartment—so much for my stupid plan of her living on her own and going to college. Alex and I were losing that special bond we had. During the arguments, he was on my side, especially when she was present. He was an honorable man and tried his best to be fair. But I saw he was disappointed in me. I was failing that "for better or for worse" promise. I struggled to define what it was that I couldn't overcome within me. He wanted me to accept all of her transgressions as normal youths' misbehavior, and something in me just couldn't do it. I decided it was time for action. I informed Alex and Julia that he and I would give her money for the first and last month's rent, plus the security deposit, plus whatever else was required, and she was moving out—immediately.

Adamantly opposed to the move, Julia insisted that she was getting used to living with us and that it was not as bad for her as it was initially, and she pledged to not overstep her boundaries anymore. Alex contended that he would feel more comfortable if she stayed with us, where she was under our control. He also said that we couldn't afford to give her such money. And then I retorted that we couldn't afford not to. So she took the money, and to my big surprise, she didn't spend it all on clothes, but actually rented a fancy apartment in a fancy area, together with her new best friend, Marina.

My relationship with Alex was damaged, and it took a few weeks for us to begin the healing process. But we loved each other, and thank goodness we valued our own life very much as well. So we reconciled, and it was like our second honeymoon, although we never had the first one.

He said I love you every time he left, kissed me again when he arrived home, and still put his hand on my shoulder in the car. Once again, I sang the same old song, "I love my life."

Alex called Julia every day to be updated on her problems.

"Julia, how are things?"

"They did it again! I came downstairs to move my car like one minute after eight o'clock, and they had given me a parking ticket already. I begged that bitch, and she was like, 'Oh yah, one minute after? Why didn't you come one minute before, honey?' They do it to me every Monday!"

"Why did you leave your car there in the evening if you knew there was going to be street cleaning the next morning?"

"Do you know what time I came home last night from the nightclub? If you came home at like four o'clock in the morning, you would know how it is to look for parking when you're ready to crash."

A week later, Alex discovered her issues had escalated even further.

"Julia, why are you not at work today?"

"I'm off today. I have to go to court. Did you forget? I told you! No? I thought I did. Those idiots, the cops, they gave me a ticket because these people were passing through the crosswalk and were like almost on the other side as I was making the turn. But those cops said they were still in the middle of the crosswalk and that I almost ran them over, which is a total lie. They just get jealous when they see someone who is young and beautiful and drives a Jaguar. So I'm going to court."

"What Jaguar? Didn't you just recently buy an old Toyota?"

"Oh that? I totaled it a month ago. Didn't I tell you? But I will most likely get some money from the girl who I collided with. Although she is like saying that it was my fault, while I am sure it was hers. So I borrowed some money and bought this very old Jaguar. It has some mechanical problems, but you should see it—classic!"

Every week there was a new disaster with her. And it was never her fault.

Alex, the trusting man that he is, would say to me, "She is such an unfortunate girl. Luck is never on her side."

Then matters abruptly came to a head.

"Now guess what happened?" Alex began. "Marina turned out to be such a complete bitch. She owes two thousand dollars to the telephone company because she was always calling her boyfriend overseas. Plus, she owes Julia another fifteen hundred dollars for her part of the rent, and now she just takes off, and this trusting, silly girl of mine is left with this huge debt."

"Let the landlord contact Marina and deal with the unpaid rent at least. She signed the contract."

"Julia put everything in her name because Marina had no credit history whatsoever. We had to sign for her."

"Who is *we*?"

"Well, as I said, Marina could not sign the papers because she didn't have any credit history—or so she said, that lying bitch. Julia does have credit history, but it's very bad. Since it was you who forced her out of our place, I had to cosign all the papers. I did it for you."

He did it for me. That was rich. That was very rich! Did he have Julia's talent of making everything somebody else's fault? Alex and Julia would make good defense attorneys—that is, if they had any brains. I attempted to estimate the damage this time.

"So what happens now?"

"We have to pay the rent, which is late, and pay the telephone company. Or she is coming back."

"I am paying the rent, and she is not coming back. I am not paying the telephone bill. Let them disconnect the telephone."

"I will go mad if I don't talk to her every day. Where will I look for her? I am doing it for myself."

At least *this* he was not doing for me.

"Here is the only deal I am going to agree on: She finds a very cheap studio apartment and lives alone within her means. Alex, how did you let all this happen to us? Where are we—you and I—in all this mess? I cannot even say a word about any of this to my family. I declared a happy ending and cannot undeclare it now."

"Vika, she was married when I met you. Who knew that her life would go in this direction?"

"Did it ever cross your mind that every time you give her money you have to multiply it by two because we have two children between the two of us? I'm writing Danny a check for the amount we spend on her."

"Nonsense, we absolutely cannot afford it. He works and makes good money. Is he late on his payments? Does he ask you for money? No. Then why should we help him?"

"How logical! Why doesn't she just do the same?"

"Because while Danny was being pampered at home reading *The Count of Monte Cristo*, Julia was living with her junkie mother not being taught good from bad and right from wrong."

"And how is that my problem now? It's her problem now. It's her problem now!"

"It's my problem, too. I'm guilty of not paying enough attention to her, although I did everything fathers not living with their kids can do. She's trying. Give her a chance. She will learn. She is a very kind and warm creature. She'll pull through."

Julia ended up moving to a small guesthouse someone was renting out, and it remained quiet for a few months. But the fact that I didn't hear the news didn't mean that there wasn't any.

Alex would come home from helping her set up her new place looking completely dejected and heartbroken. "You should see what a dump she is living in. How can people even consider renting out a place like that? What greed can do to some people! The only reason Julia rented it was that the price, of course, is very cheap. How can a young, weak woman survive in this country?"

"I was alone when I came here and when Danny went to live with his father. I paid him as much child support as I could, but not too much, I am afraid. I starved, but I had my priorities. First, I put aside money for the apartment, then for gas to drive to work, and then for all the rest. So sometimes what I had left wasn't enough to cover food, for example—or white boots."

"How can you compare yourself to her? You're a strong, educated woman with a profession. But she…she never had to work with that son of a bitch of a husband who spoiled her rotten with the good life, never encouraged her to work, and kept her all for himself."

"Is it ever her fault? Ever? In anything? How can you be so blind when it comes to her? Double standards—they suck."

"Victoria, it's called *unconditional love*. That's how parents love their children."

"No, no, no, there's no such thing. And if there is, it's wrong. You can help bail out your children of any mess, but you don't have to pretend that a mess is not a mess. No love can force you to call *wrong right*. Someday, it can end very tragically."

"Victoria, you're not a human being—at least not a woman. Maybe this is why your son hates you."

This wasn't the first time he'd hurt me like that, as I am sure you've noticed.

"I don't care if he loves me or hates me," I lied. I lied badly. "But, most importantly, I did pay attention to him when he was growing up and taught him to be a good student, to do his duties, to read books, to understand art, travel—the real values, not designer clothes. And, to think, I even went as far as forcing him to clean his room so it would become routine for him in his daily life. I annoyed him by lecturing all the time about good versus evil. I will never bury the corpse for him, if you know what I mean. I pray I'll never have to. But if it comes to that, I'll tell him, 'What you did was wrong,' and help him face the consequences. And if he hates me for that, so be it. Although I'm sure he won't."

Those were long and sickening arguments. In the beginning, we grew together because we spoke the same language. And now we were growing apart because we no longer spoke the same language.

But, as it happened more than once, when I felt as if there was no going any further, Alex would wake up, so to speak, from all that and frantically try to start fixing things between us. Julia would continue being Julia, but Alex would start talking to her in a different tone, scolding her as fathers do. He would complain to me about her, and I would give him advice to help her with things, and our love would be somewhat repaired. In my mind, all could be forgotten if he would just admit that all of this was wrong, and then I would help him straighten it out. I will put up with anything; just don't make me look like an idiot by insulting my intelligence.

I frequently wondered how our marriage would differ if not for this horrible burden. And I am sure it would be as happy as a marriage can be in the real world. Alex was a dream husband, and I am not exaggerating. If only we had met twenty years before and had a life together with our common children. If only—I always despised people for making this kind of pathetic remark. There is no such thing as *if only*.

They say that there is no such thing as a second marriage, either, that there are always the two unsolvable problems: the money and the children. But despite all that, Alex was the closest person I ever had—ever. I cannot explain how we managed to have all those disagreements and still stay together, and even have a marriage happy in general. I learned to compartmentalize. There were perpetual troubles with Julia, but there was also the unique world we shared—our togetherness. We took it seriously, and we tried hard. That's how the first three years of our marriage passed. One of the things that kept me sane was my old friend, Belka. All right, it's time to introduce you to Belka.

CHAPTER 13
BELKA

Belka's name is actually Bella, the Italian word meaning "beauty." But for all us old friends who knew each other forever, she was Belka. Also, in Russian, the word *belka* means "squirrel." So we, her friends, decided we liked her better as a squirrel than as a beauty. That's what friends are for, aren't they?

She and I went to college together, we worked together, and we raised our children together; we did everything together before we came to the Sates. I know everything about her, and she knows everything about me. I don't have to explain anything to Belka because she just understands.

When Alex moved in with me, Belka made it her business to fly here from the East Coast to see for herself what I was up to. Before she left, she imparted her satisfaction—as if I needed her blessing. Honestly, it meant a lot to me. Just don't tell her. Usually, we talk about everything and nothing. We just like to contact each other; it's like a reward after a difficult week or a problem.

When this extravaganza with Julia started, Belka would call and quietly listen. I knew she had nothing to say because nobody would have anything to say in this situation. Maybe a psychiatrist would, but Belka was much cheaper, especially if she was the one who had called long distance.

It was amazing how she intuitively knew when I needed her to call. She would call and simply say, "What?"

"Hi, Belka, good evening to you, too. How are you?"

"I'm fine, thanks for asking. Enough about me. What is it now? I cannot leave you for a second."

And if she were in trouble, I would do the same for her as well. I always did and always will, and so will she. We never talk about it; we just know.

CHAPTER 14
MORE NEWS

One night, an anonymous caller urgently asked to speak to Mr. Alex Lansky. Alex replied with "This is he," and we learned that the person calling was a policeman. He phoned because they had received a distress call from Julia screaming about somebody trying to break in and hearing voices. When they arrived at her place, she claimed she could hear her mother crying for help. We got very scared, as we knew her mother was overseas and didn't understand what was happening. The policeman indicated that either they would take her in and decide what to do with her or we had to immediately take her into our care. Of course, we rushed there and brought her home. We could not imagine what was wrong.

Late in the night, Julia started crying out in pain and proclaiming she had such severe stomach pangs that she was dying. She went to our medicine cabinet and swallowed a handful of painkillers, but the pain did not stop. We grabbed her and rushed to the emergency room. After waiting for a few hours, she was finally taken back to an exam room.

An hour later, the doctor showed up and broke the news, along with our hearts and our lives. He advised us that Julia was hallucinating on drugs. He said she had developed some sort of schizophrenia that might go away if she stayed sober—only time would tell.

My mind was in a fog. I couldn't even comprehend the terms. First of all, my English vocabulary didn't previously contain the word *sober*, which I was eventually able to figure out. Then I couldn't understand what *relapse* meant in this situation, although I knew the word. A few days later, only someone who was better educated about drugs could explain it to me.

Then the doctor said they could keep her and transfer her to a psychiatric institution, but they needed her consent, and she was not cooperating. Actually, she was just out of this world. I begged the doctor to keep her for a few days until we could talk some sense into her, but he kept reiterating that they couldn't keep her against her will.

When Julia came out of the exam room, I delivered the news to her that we were leaving her there for treatment. In a zombie-like trance, she mumbled, "No." I begged her again, and she whispered, "Yes." As soon as Julia said yes, the doctor, who was watching our entire exchange, called the medical personnel to take her in. When she saw them, she screamed, "Nooooooooooo," and started to run from the room. I grabbed her, and we fell to the floor and started wrestling. The security guards were watching us intently, but they weren't allowed to interfere. I yelled to Alex to help me restrain her, but he sat with his hands over his face, and I wasn't sure whether he was crying or unconscious.

Finally, she gave up and was taken inside. She continued screaming, and she was begging me and cursing me. I will never forget that scene. I felt that I had betrayed her and that she would never forgive me. It broke my heart, because when she was in normal condition, she could be such a sweet girl.

The next day, we knew nothing of her whereabouts. A day later, she called, and with a very weak and sick voice, she asked us to come visit her at the facility. When we arrived and she was called to come see us, we didn't recognize her. She was quiet and calm and very sad. We were ready for anything, but not this. She thanked us for saving her and said she would be forever grateful to me for forcing her to get help. She understood what grief she had caused us, and from then on, she swore to follow the road to redemption.

I probably don't strike you as a very kind person, but as a matter of fact, I am. At any given point in time, I maintain the utmost compassion for others. Now, seeing her so low, I would do anything for her. I promised we would be there for her for as long as it took her to climb out of that black hole. She admitted wrong was wrong, and as I said before, that was all I needed to move past the incident. This condition met, I could do wonders to help. She would remain at the psychiatric hospital for another few days, and then she was being transferred to rehab. I know you may lose your patience with me if I tell you that I never heard that word before, but well, I'm guilty. I came from a world where we don't even hear about or know of somebody who actually does drugs. Come to think of it, I cannot believe it myself. But I am telling you the truth. There are only two possibilities: Either no one did drugs in the Soviet Union or it was never publicized. I think it was partially both. Also, if you couldn't obtain a chicken, how could you obtain drugs? It has probably changed now.

So she went to rehab for thirty days and was being a good girl. We bought her a calling card, and she called us constantly. She sounded very sweet and attentive—and very sorry. I couldn't believe it was our Julia. I suspected that all her aggressive and foolish behavior was based solely on the fact that she was always on some drug—maybe not heavily, maybe only slightly, if there were such a thing.

Julia had left a pack of cigarettes at our place, and Alex, who used to smoke when he was young, started smoking again just to comfort himself. I tried to smoke, too, but it was too disgusting. He mentioned in passing that she also left a pack of lighter menthol cigarettes that I would probably find less horrible, and I have no idea how it happened, but we both started smoking as a result.

Every evening, we would walk around the block just to get out of the house, often stopping at the pet store around the corner to mindlessly stare at the tropical fish or lovebirds or snakes. We would stand there for hours like two zombies, not talking and not thinking. I have hated pet stores ever since; every time I pass one I feel that despair all over again. Everything in life lost its meaning. Nothing mattered anymore. I used to get so excited to buy new clothes or go to the movies or attend some party. Now everything was put in a different perspective. As for meeting with friends and family, I was too proud to admit—except to Belka—that I failed—again.

Some two weeks into those blessed thirty days that Julia was supposed to stay at the rehab facility, she called to convey that she felt absolutely normal and that she would not stay there for another minute with all those "low-life people." That's exactly what she said: "I am not staying here. They all are low-life junkies."

My heart stopped. "And how do you think you're different?"

"I won't listen to talk like that. I am coming, and you cannot stop me."

"Coming where?"

"To my father's place. I have a father, you know."

Our good old Julia was back—figuratively and literally.

She came home, and we all acted as if nothing had happened. We quite honestly didn't know how else to deal with the situation. Alex and I immediately went about collecting all of our medicine and liquor and hiding it in storage, as we were afraid she might start looking for it.

I tried pretending that I went into hibernation, a deep, lethargic sleep, and waited for better times to wake up. On top of everything, Alex was sent to Las Vegas for a few months to work on some construction site. He would leave home during the week and come back on the weekends. So then I smoked without Alex; it obviously became more than social smoking.

While Julia was "recuperating," she slept all day long and went out at night, falling into much the same pattern as before. She was dating a guy from showbiz she had met in rehab. He was so cool he even managed to obtain drugs in rehab, which explained the sudden change in Julia's behavior at the facility—the return of her old aggression. They fell in love there, and he treated her generously. Can anybody tell me how it's possible to buy drugs while in rehab? I'm sure you don't know, either.

Meanwhile, I began developing some very strange symptoms where sudden, severe bouts of dizziness would overpower me, causing me to nearly collapse. It was as if a few times a day my body could not stay upright. I was scared; I was preparing to die. I started going to see one doctor after another. I remember one Sunday when Alex asked me if I could take Julia to see a psychiatrist that Monday since he was leaving again for Las Vegas. I apprised him that I had an important medical procedure at the hospital myself. As it happened, I was scheduled for a brain MRI at the UCLA Medical Center. I didn't relate to him how serious I thought my health issues were and how scared I was to undergo that procedure the following day. The result of that test meant a life or death sentence to me. When I gave him my excuse, I hoped he would be scared for me, perhaps even as scared as he was when Julia was in danger. But he was so overwhelmed with all of his own problems that he forgot to worry about me, too.

He said, "Don't worry, dear, I'll ask somebody else to take her to her appointment. You do your things."

He never thought to inquire as to what doctor I was seeing or what my problem was.

The next day, right before the technician shoveled me into that casket, I cried inconsolably. I felt so sorry for myself. There I was, alone and unsure of what to expect. I didn't say anything about it to my parents because I didn't want to cause them extraneous apprehension or stress at their age. I didn't mention anything to Greg and Nelly, either, because I was too proud to admit that my marriage was bordering on a fiasco. Plus, my sister-in-law would undoubtedly blab all about the details to everyone, which I was not ready for yet. I also didn't share anything with Danny because I was so afraid that he wouldn't pay attention to what I was saying. So I convinced myself that I just didn't want to burden him with worries about me. I drove myself to the hospital and had no idea how I would get back home after everything was said and done. But, first, I had to survive the test—or rather, the results.

I called Alex just to hear his voice.

He picked up the phone after the first ring and sounded alarmed. "Vika, what is it? Is it Julia? Did you hear from her? What did her doctor say? Did they do a drug test on her?"

"Nothing like that, don't worry," I replied nonchalantly. "I haven't heard from her yet."

I hung up.

He forgot to worry about me, too; he even forgot I was in the hospital. He was the best husband I ever had, which wasn't hard by a long shot, but he wasn't concerned whether I had a brain tumor. How was that possible? Oh, yes, that's right, I didn't fill him in on the details. I couldn't bear to see Alex pretending to be heartbroken for me, while, in actuality, he was only worried about Julia's drug test. Also, in my heart of hearts, I knew that if all this horror weren't happening with his daughter, he would be genuinely sick with worry for me. It was just that his limits couldn't cover us both.

The technician noticed me crying before he put me into that box and regarded my brave expression in the face of death after he pulled me back out, so he took mercy on me and looked at the films. Even though the doctor still had to study everything very thoroughly, he affirmed that, from his many years of experience, it looked like I had no problems—zilch, zero, nada. Now I will tell you what I felt at that moment: I felt such relief, such overpowering relief, and I also felt such disappointment.

I don't know how Sigmund Freud or any other famous psychiatrist would explain it, but I felt slightly discontented. The night before, I lay in bed envisioning how heartbroken Alex would be to lose me. He no doubt would have many candidates to take my place because he was so gorgeous and manly, but while with any of them, he would always remember me, and not one of them would be as special to him as I had been. Then he would know! And any one of them would have to have Julia thrust upon them as part of the two-for-one deal as well. That thought made me feel somewhat better.

Moreover, I pictured Danny coming to my deathbed and finally expressing how much he loved me and how much he would miss me. I would tell him that I loved him more than anything else in the world and that I forgave him. And I would ask him to forgive me. I wept all night long envisioning all those beautiful, melodramatic scenes; I pitied myself tremendously.

And there I was, not dying. But don't get me wrong—relief was the strongest sensation of all. I also was going to see a doctor in a week, and if he told me that I was, indeed, healthy…

On the way home, I called Belka. She was aware of everything, of course. And, unlike the others, she was really worried, but pretending not to care too much, so as not to scare me.

"How did it go?"

"Belka, I just had that test. I will tell you all about it in a week when I see my doctor."

A week later, I met with my famous neurologist in Beverly Hills. He confirmed I had no brain tumor or anything of the sort. He was convinced that the spells I was having were the result of severe anxiety, for which he would prescribe me medication.

"Belka, it's all over. I'm healthy as a horse, after all. I'm simply a neurotic wreck."

"Aren't we all…aren't we all…Oh my God, thank goodness! Neurotic, erotic—who cares? Vika, we still have many, many years to joke! Just don't you ever scare me like this again, you idiot."

I went home with resolutions.

I called Danny and left him a message that I loved him more than anything else in the world—just like that, not afraid that he would be annoyed by it. Then I contacted Julia's landlord, and she gave me some discounts and agreed to let me pay the outstanding rent in a few installments. I packed all of Julia's stuff and drove it to her guesthouse. It was Friday, and Alex was coming home for the weekend. In the evening, when I saw both of them, I announced that either Julia alone or both of them—whatever they preferred—had to move out of my place. They would have to choose which it would be. Alex always sensed when I was getting close to the point of no return. He made the decision to stick with me and let Julia go.

My last resolution was to quit smoking.

Thus concluded another stage of my "happily ever after."

෯

CHAPTER 15
NEW HOUSE

After five years of this turbulence, we managed to reach some kind of stability again. We became closer, in a sense, but we lost that intense passion we used to share. I only hoped it would miraculously reemerge one day. Alex and I became pals, travel companions, and a small corporation with our own business affairs. Our condo lost its charm for me; it was infected with all that horror. It was polluted with things that didn't belong in my world, so I decided we had to move. I told Alex I wanted to buy a house. Alex was absolutely against it, but as usual, he gave in to my crazy drive. I found a house close to where we both worked; we sold the condo and became homeowners.

Alex hated it very much at first. But, little by little, it became our baby, our common child we never had, and in time, we both learned to love it very much. Alex, being an incredibly responsible and organized person, made the place look like a dollhouse. We were so proud of it; we showed it off to anybody who cared to look. It was very modest compared to our friends' houses, but as everything in our marriage, we valued even the things other people neglected to notice. I knew nothing about plants and gardening, yet I determinedly planted a small garden, and Alex complimented me on it every time he passed it. My house was my castle—untainted and sacred.

We experienced a few bumps in the beginning as we were getting accustomed to being proud landowners, homeowners, garage owners, leaky-roof owners, and even our very own security system owners. We installed the system not only to protect our not-very-valuable valuables, but also mainly to have a fire alarm for when we went out of town on the weekends or out of the country on vacation. Thus the alarm system was supposed to provide us with some peace of mind. But it ended up giving us some headaches instead—at least initially. We always remembered to activate it upon departure, but sometimes forgot to deactivate it when returning home. A minute after we had returned and forgot to disarm the system, the security company would call to ask for the password and whether everything was all right. We would apologize, ask them not to dispatch the police, and promise not to trigger the alarm the next time.

Alex went to work very early, so I was usually the one to set the alarm, and he was the one to turn it off. Every morning, I would deftly punch in our code and leave. It became our routine.

One weekend, Alex worked two nights in a row, as they were finishing a big project at the hospital, so he came home at 7:00 a.m. on Monday morning and went straight to bed. I tried to be very quiet while getting ready for work. I had my breakfast as usual, got my purse as usual, opened the garage door as usual, and set the alarm as usual. Half an hour later, Alex woke up to go to the bathroom and went back to sleep. Our alarm system detected his motion in the hallway, and a minute later, the security company called our home to verify what was going on. But, reasonably, Alex didn't want to start any phone conversations since he still had a good six hours to sleep. After not getting a response from our home, they called my cell phone. I heard the phone ring, but I was on my way to work and couldn't answer while driving. (Don't get me wrong,

I do have a Bluetooth device, but it's still sitting in our kitchen cabinet. I will install it one of these days.) I didn't think twice about not answering my cell phone, as I was sure any call could wait until I parked; it would only be my mom or Belka at that time of the day, anyway. But the cell phone persisted ringing nonstop. I grabbed the phone. I didn't recognize the first number; the next few missed calls were from Greg's cell phone.

I dialed back and barked, "This better be important. I'm on the freeway right now, and you're calling like crazy."

Greg replied, "Vika, your security company called me. They detected somebody walking inside your house. They called your home phone and your cell, but nobody answered. Then they called me since I am your next point of contact. I tried to call your cell, but you didn't answer, so they sent the police to investigate. I think there's a robbery going on at your house right now. Don't go back home because it might be dangerous. Let the police take care of it. Do you want me to drive over there?"

"Greg, I'm turning back right now! Please, come over as fast as you can, and *please*, don't let them shoot Alex!"

"Is Alex home now? What's going on?"

"Never mind, just don't let them shoot Alex. And don't let him shoot them! I'm the one who deserves to be shot."

At that very minute, a very suspenseful action movie was unfolding at my house. The police arrived, and two policemen knocked loudly on the front door. Alex woke up and was livid that the solicitors had become so annoying. He found the earplugs I use, which are stored in the drawer of my nightstand by the bed, and tried to go back to sleep. But he was too infuriated to calm down that easily. The knocking finally abated, and through the bedroom shutters, he saw their silhouettes peeking in the windows. Then they began knocking on the windows. Poor Alex—he went from dazed and confused to hyper alert in two seconds. First, he grabbed his gun from under the bed and then grabbed the phone and dialed 911. He reported a home invasion, and they instructed him to sit still and not come into contact with the intruders until the police arrived. Then they asked him whether he had a gun at home, to which he responded that he had a gun collection. They told him they were sending national guardsmen and cautioned him to lay low and wait for them to arrive.

By the time I got there, there were two police cars, a fire truck, an ambulance, a news van, numerous policemen, firefighters, medical personnel, and neighbors—and Nelly. She had to be the first to know everything so that, later, she could tell everybody and give her own interpretation of what happened.

The policemen, who came first, broke the glass in our front door, opened it, and entered the house.

I ran from my car toward my surrounded house scream-ing, "Don't shoot! Don't shoot! Alex, don't be afraid. I'm here!" They made an effort to stop me, but try to stop me when my Alex is in danger. I shouted to the policemen that it was I who activated the alarm.

Greg finally arrived and ran to me. Alex, wearing only his briefs, stood in the entryway holding his gun. His face expressed such outrage; he still had no clue what all the ruckus was about. I reassured the first policemen I came to that everything was all right and that we would gladly pay any fine for the false alarm that caused the police dispatch. I also notified the national guardsmen that it was a false alarm, and I implored a shocked Alex to nod in agreement. I saw the media van and Nelly leaving first; they were enormously dis-appointed—no shooting, no adultery, not even a cat stuck in a tree. Then all the others started pulling away, too. Once all the commotion had subsided, the policemen had me sign some papers acknowledging the incident as a false alarm.

My usually very self-controlled Alex quietly, but firmly, asked me if I knew what had just happened. I explained to him that I had activated the alarm system before I left for work, and after he went to the bathroom, all hell broke loose. He looked at me and looked at me some more (sometimes he can be very slow), trying to put the pieces together. Then he screamed and grabbed me by the neck, or maybe he just wanted to hug me, I don't know. He probably didn't know himself. He just needed to relieve himself; he was on the verge of doing something crazy.

Greg was so afraid that Alex would strangle me (I would if I were him) that he grabbed Alex, and they started fighting. But, thank goodness, Alex quickly came to his senses. He said he needed a drink. He and Greg went into the kitchen and both had a big glass of tequila for breakfast. I begged him to forgive me, but Greg told me to get lost or go to work and leave the men to do their thing. I never asked what exactly that was. Later that day, Greg called to let me know it was safe to return home.

For a long time after that memorable morning, I had nightmares, especially after eating late, that police were breaking into our house, and they saw my Alex standing there pointing the gun at them and…Who knows what could happen next? Maybe the fact that he wore nothing but his briefs would save him? Would a robber be wearing briefs unless he decided to steal them and was trying them on?

Alex printed out a big sign and taped it to the door leading into the garage:

VICTORIA!!! CONCENTRATE!!!

CHAPTER 16
PARIS

One more advantage of selling the condo was having some leftover money to take a vacation. We had postponed our honeymoon indefinitely, and finally, we could afford to go away together. We both loved to travel. It was absolutely impossible, however, to travel behind the Iron Curtain, so all immigrants who come from the Soviet Union are heavy travelers. It's like forbidden fruit to us.

We didn't even have to discuss where to go. Where are first-time travelers and second-time honeymooners supposed to go? Paris, baby! We managed to book a very cheap trip, and then we found ourselves in Paris in the middle of October. The weather was probably not suitable for other tourists, but to us, everything was just pure joy.

We would wake up early; put on sneakers, raincoats, and hats; take our huge umbrella; and head off to explore Paris. During the course of my life, I had read so much about Paris that I recognized the names of streets and historic sites, yet I had envisioned everything differently. Now, in person, Paris looked much less grandiose and magnificent, but much warmer, friendlier, and dirtier. I was disappointed for the first two days; then once I changed my perception of it, I just loved it.

We walked from early in the morning till late at night. Alex patiently went through all the mandatory points of interest from my Michelin travel book that I imposed upon us. And once we were done with all the two- and three-star sites from the book, we started to really enjoy Paris. We just walked and walked and ate baguettes with bologna and drank real coffee. We walked some more and kissed as if we really were young honeymooners. And, in the evening, we lay in each other's arms in our tiny bed in our tiny room gazing at the illuminated, lacy Eiffel Tower through the window.

We spent very little money. In the following years, we took much more expensive vacations, but still, this vacation was the most memorable. Our future was looking up; I counted my blessings. How lucky I was that this very worthy man loved me.

When we returned home, Alex bypassed checking our messages until the next morning because he wanted to prolong our holiday. This simple action prompted the return of that hateful, sickening feeling of instability. I had momentarily forgotten our learned habit of looking at each other when the phone rang, as if asking each other to answer and face the consequences. But, by then, Alex was my best friend, and I was behind him unconditionally—on one condition. He was supposed to call bad, bad and good, good. And he was trying.

Another two years passed in that manner. Julia occasionally gave us problems. Like the time when her car was towed away and she needed a mere $400 to get it back. Or the time she gave some money to a girlfriend who couldn't pay her rent because she lost big in Las Vegas, and then she called us because she had no money to pay her own rent.

When we lectured her about handing out money to somebody else despite having none for herself, she said, "I can't believe how selfish you are! My friend's problem is my problem!"

In an attempt to reason with her, I said, "But, in the end, we're the ones who paid Mary's rent, aren't we?"

"No, it was me who helped Mary. As for you, you just helped me with my rent, as all parents do."

You couldn't win an argument with Julia.

One evening, she came to visit and declared, "I decided to become an actress."

Of course, what else would an airheaded and cute creature living so close to Hollywood like to become?

She continued, "Knowing you, I won't ask you for the money. All I ask is that you cosign the loan for the school that somebody highly recommended to me. It costs twelve thousand dollars a year, and they tell me that everybody becomes a star after graduating from there."

I saw Alex desperately trying to formulate an excuse.

"Why don't you take out the loan yourself?" I suggested. "Why do you need us?"

"If I had credit like you two do, I would never ask you. I knew you would give me a hard time. You are the most negative person I've ever seen in my life, Victoria. If I were your own daughter, wouldn't you be happy to help me succeed and become a superstar?"

"A superstar, no less? Would you settle for a medium-sized star? Are you also required to have some talent for that school, or is twelve thousand dollars a year sufficient? Also, considering the interest, it's much more than that. How many years does it take to become a star?"

"Papa, talk to me! I don't want to listen to her! I'm not asking you for the money; all I need is your freaking signature!"

I pressed on, "Julia, if you had ever taken out a loan, you would know that if the borrower doesn't pay, it becomes the responsibility of the cosigner. We worked very hard to build our excellent credit and our less than excellent savings. You go ahead and do the same."

"You know I'll pay on time! I calculated everything, and I can do it! I've been working at this new place for almost four months now, and my boss adores me! I'll be promoted to manager soon, I can tell. And if I miss like a payment or two and you have to help me out, you know I'm good for it."

"But you've never paid us back before. Why would this time be different?"

"Papa!"

"All right, Julia, I will go with you to see that school this weekend, and then we'll decide what to do," Alex finally retorted.

By the time the weekend rolled around, Julia lost interest in that particular school. In the meantime, she met somebody who had graduated from the school and didn't become a movie star. Apparently, when he applied, they promised find him a good job. Then after he graduated, they weren't interested in him anymore.

She was outraged. "Just think of it! He paid all that money for the school, and now he like actually has to look for a job! It's a good thing we didn't fall for it, too. Those crooks!"

Alex was visibly relieved. "See, you always worry right away," he said to me. "We got away easy this time."

"Don't you think you should explain to her that you have to look for a job by yourself, along with all other things in life?"

"Vika, weren't you young and silly once upon a time?"

"She is twenty-seven years old. She is not that young anymore. In fact, you're twenty-seven years late already. Did you teach her anything at all when she was a child? Or did you think that since she was such a cute little girl she didn't have to play by the rules?"

"What do you want from me? I will never ever abandon my daughter!"

So we went back to a semi-normal routine. Julia continued working at that office and unabatedly suggested that she would become a manager in the near future. I didn't want to aggravate Alex, so I didn't dare ask manager of what she was about to become.

He remarked about her sharp appearance and attire as well as her expert typing skills. According to him, she was even responsible for training a new hire to enter patient files into the computer. Alex was not good with computers, so those sitting at the computers and even typing something always impressed him. Julia showed him around the office and introduced him to her coworkers, and he commented on how friendly and cordial the staff members were and the complimentary things they had to say about Julia.

Alex called his sister, Kathy, and said, "I visited Julia at work today. What do you mean what work? She's been working at a doctor's office for a few months already. Her position? She works on the computer. And is she typing really fast! She's always been a bright girl. And she is already kind of a manager, too. I saw the girl she gives assignments to, and she might have a few more."

After he hung up, I jokingly asked, "Can you raise the bar for her?"

"Not all children have to be doctors or lawyers. Somebody has to be an office manager, too."

Aha, that's what her position was going to be when she grows up—office manager. She will manage staplers.

He went on, "As long as she is not on drugs, I am proud of her, whatever it may be."

CHAPTER 17
MEDITERRANEAN BLAST

One more year passed. Julia met yet another love of her life. Usually, we had some kind of a break when that happened, and we could afford to take a vacation for a week or two. She was always an albatross around someone's neck—if not someone else's, it was ours. Although we never admitted it to each other, we felt relieved every time she dated somebody.

We had never taken a cruise before, as it was not our idea of a vacation; we thought it was not active enough for us. But all our friends were crazy about cruises, so we decided to give it a try. I found a good deal online and booked a two-week Mediterranean cruise. Alex insisted it was too expensive and encouraged me to find a shorter and cheaper cruise. But I reasoned that since we had to fly so far and would lose a few days to jetlag, it didn't make sense to go for only one week. In our family, I usually won arguments; I think Alex conceded to picking his battles. He frequently joked, "The last word is always mine—'Yes, ma'am.'"

It was still a whole month until the cruise day, and I was enjoying the best part of any vacation—the anticipation. And right after I booked this trip, I caught a cold that developed into an ear infection. It was very painful, but the most painful thing was the fear of it ruining our vacation. I went to see a doctor, who prescribed me some antibiotics. I took them for almost three weeks and actually overdosed on them—but we learned that later. At the time, we thought it was some kind of bacteria or something like that. It upset my stomach to the point where I went to the bathroom every few minutes, and every time, there was blood. Two days before our vacation, I went to the hospital for a series of tests, and the doctor absolutely prohibited me to fly while I was bleeding so badly until we knew the test results—a week later! I was supposed to be in Europe a week later! I was very unwell, but it was nothing compared to the fact that we had to cancel our vacation. And, senselessly, I hadn't purchased travel insurance, so we were losing an unthinkable amount of money.

I am sharing all these personal details with you so that you can admire Alex's behavior, which was indeed admirable. In this abnormal situation, he behaved like a man. First of all, he was so worried about me that he ignored all my protests and accompanied me to the bathroom to see whether I was doing better. He called all the time from work to check on me, which was very unusual for him. When he works, he works, and you don't mess with his work. He went to the pharmacy multiple times a day whenever anybody recommended something else. He made sure I was drinking plenty of Gatorade and not eating solid food. *And he told me not to worry about losing all that money, that enormous sum.* Most importantly, I knew he meant it. He said all that mattered was my getting better, and I saw he was fighting back tears as he was telling me this. Oh God, he did love me! Later, when I ever needed the proof of it, I remembered him crying when I was sick.

The night before our scheduled flight, Alex packed for both of us while I lay in bed. One of the bags was filled with only Gatorade—twenty-eight bottles, two bottles per day. We went to sleep not knowing whether we would leave the next day or stay home. In the morning, I decided I couldn't do it to us and that I was willing to take a chance. I couldn't carry anything; poor Alex had to drag all our luggage by himself.

When we entered our cabin on the ship, he opened the safe, put the twenty-eight bottles of Gatorade in it, and said, "I'm so glad you have something to eat for the rest of the vacation." It sounded so funny, considering the endless amount of food available around the clock on the ship. I tried not to eat or drink anything but Gatorade, which allowed us to enjoy a very good vacation. On shore, we went to eat at some famous restaurants; Alex enjoyed the food, and I just sampled it and spat it out. Alex laughed at me and joked that we had to tell them that I didn't like anything I tried so they would reimburse us. When I remember that incident, I always feel warm and nostalgic. I was so loved; somebody worried about me so much. I was not spoiled with things like that before.

Oh Alex, my Alex.

CHAPTER 18
FAMILY THANKSGIVING

Every year we gather at Greg's for Thanksgiving. Nelly is the world's expert at making turkey taste very delicious, which is almost impossible. As usual, I was assigned to unsophisticated side dishes—salads and mashed potatoes. So that morning I went to the produce market to buy the necessary ingredients. Distracted by my intense concentration on picking the best veggies that would deserve a spot of honor alongside Nelly's turkey, I didn't notice the approaching figure, and all of a sudden, somebody grabbed my arm. It was Nelly's sister, Sofia, who had startled me. I always liked her a lot and was glad to see her.

She and her family had just come to America two years earlier, as they had been refused permission to leave the Soviet Union for fifteen years by the Russian authorities. Her husband was a scientist and probably knew something that America was not yet supposed to know. After they had applied for permission to leave Russia, he was fired from his job and worked as a janitor for years. Nelly and Sofia's parents were heartbroken, and every time I saw them after moving to America, they would always half-jokingly say, "It should be Sofia to come here before you. You never wanted it too much, anyway."

Their father worked for ten years after they arrived in the United States, which was very unusual for older people, who could just collect a pension and all the benefits without going to work. He was a great engineer in Russia, and here, he worked for a small engineering company for all ten of his working years. The owner treasured him and begged him to work at least part time when he retired, so he continued working two days a week. Their mother didn't work and kept herself busy by collecting and sending parcels to Sofia and her family back in Russia.

Their father died first. He dropped dead of a heart attack right at the office. Their mother outlived him by a couple of years. She had cancer, and her only hope was to live to see her Sofia come here. Now and then, after visiting my parents, I would stop by to say hello to her. They lived in the area where all elderly Russian people lived. She was so pleasant and brave, never overwhelming anybody with her misfortunes. Sometimes, she called Sofia when I was there, and we all talked, the three of us. Once, she revealed to me, "We saved some money for the girls. I know Nelly and Greg are doing very well and don't need our money, but to be fair and not foster contention between the sisters, we decided to give each of them half of what we have. Nelly will find how to use it, I'm sure. As for Sofia, when she comes here and has nothing, it will be a lifesaver. I only hope it will help them. What else could her dad and I do for them?"

Another time, she asked, "Vika, can you do me a huge favor and pass this ring to Sofia when you see her? I saw it at the jewelry store, and I just loved it. I wish I had it when I was young. It's Sofia's birthstone. I want her to have it. I miss her terribly and want her to wear it every day of her life. And, dear, promise not to say anything about it to Nelly."

"Aunty Mary," I replied, "you put me in an awkward situation. I don't want to be a part of any conspiracy against my brother and his wife."

"Nelly has everything she needs and more. I would give it to her to pass to Sofia, but she will feel she is being treated unfairly. I don't know why, but this is how she will feel, I know. Please, do me this favor. You don't have to lie about not having it. You just don't have to mention it. Is that lying?" Then she repeated a few times, "I only hope they will not have to go through what we went through…."

Unwillingly, I agreed. When Sofia finally came here with her family, the first thing I did was I went to greet them and get rid of that ring. She was so touched and so thankful. Her mother had been dead for a year by then.

After they came to America, I saw them only a few times at Greg's. And then they stopped going there. Knowing Nelly's exacting character, I assumed they had an argument, and it was a pity because I liked their clean-cut family a lot.

So I was glad to bump into her that morning.

"Victoria, what are you doing here so early?"

"I'm getting ready for tonight. I'll see you and your gang tonight, I guess?"

"No, we're not coming. We were invited elsewhere."

"Are you kidding me? You cannot miss your sister's famous turkey. Nobody can match her—nobody."

"We'll have to pass. I'm not sure I'm ready to see her yet."

It sounded like the opening to a conversation for which I was supposed to make further inquiries, but I was afraid to do so. Don't I have to be on my brother's side no matter what? She waited for me to draw her out, and since I remained quiet, she continued.

"Vika, since you were involved in this from the beginning [oh no, not the ring story, please], I want to tell you what it's all about. My parents left me and Nelly some money—forty thousand dollars to be exact. Since we had no American social security number, being in Russia, they had no way of leaving my share to me legally—or at least they didn't know how. So they gave all forty thousand dollars to Nelly and told her that half of it is for her family and half is for mine. My mom called me very often, you know. She told me about it a million times so I knew that twenty thousand dollars was waiting for me here if I ever came.

"Now, Nelly—who did all the work of obtaining our immigration papers, paying to sponsor our coming here, and so on—gave me ten thousand and said that's what our parents left for me. After paying her back for what she paid for our coming here from this ten thousand, we have only a few thousand left, which cannot even buy us a used car. I know nobody helped them when they came, and I know we will have to work hard to establish ourselves here. And so we will. But to think that my only sister could jeopardize losing me for the lousy ten thousand dollars she decided to keep is appalling. You could say that I am jeopardizing losing her for the same ten thousand dollars, too, but it's different. Do you see the difference? She is risking losing me for the ten thousand dollars, whereas I am risking losing her by not accepting the fact that she was ready to lose me for the lousy ten thousand dollars. I know I'm not really making any sense here. But do you understand? Do you see what I mean?"

"Yes, I see."

"Oh, thank you. It's so important to me that you understand what I'm talking about. I've read a million books with stories of when poor relatives become jealous and mean and ungrateful to their rich, charitable relatives. And when these noble, helpful, rich people need help themselves, they are sold out by those whom they helped because of lifelong jealousy. But I've never ever heard about a rich sister stealing money from the poor one. How do you explain that?"

"Sofia, I know what you're talking about, but I don't know what to say. I cannot take sides in this situation. Does Greg know anything about it?"

"I don't know. Probably not. He's always treated me so kindly. I don't think he's part of it. It's between me and her."

"I hope so. Nelly is the one who controls their finances. He's just required to make good money."

"I wish my parents had left this money with you. It would have been safer."

"I'm so glad they didn't. I wouldn't have even taken it. Greg is one of the very few things in my life that I will never jeopardize. I'm sorry it had to happen that way. I wish your parents didn't have any money at all. In that case, we would celebrate Thanksgiving together tonight—the whole extended family."

But then I thought better of that comment. A person who is ready to sell you out will do it again and again. Although, maybe not. Maybe when money is involved, people lose perspective. I would have to think about it.

"In the meantime," I said, "Sofia, I can lend you some money to help you make ends meet. I cannot do ten thousand, but I can give you five. You can pay it back when you're able to do so."

"Thank you, dear, but I never borrow money. We'll survive. Neiman is finally working. I will always remember that you offered, though."

The whole situation overwhelmed me so much that I forgot to buy beef tomatoes, which were a special request by Nelly.

I couldn't clear my head for the rest of the day. I went over the circumstances again and again in my mind, trying to explain things differently. It would be so much easier if Sofia were wrong or even dishonest, but I knew that wasn't the case; I myself was present during her conversations with her mother. Perhaps Nelly's manipulative behavior caused her to lie when the scenarios in her head didn't match up with the real-life situations. How could even grown-ups lie so often?

I said nothing of it to Alex. You always have to hear both sides of the argument to understand the conflict, but I hoped I would never have to hear the other side.

Later that afternoon, Alex and I went to pick up my parents. On our way out to the car, I carried their stuff, Alex helped my father, and my mom ran (on her terms) to open the car door for my father so that if, during the next thirty seconds, a sudden gust of wind, rain, hurricane, earthquake, or tsunami were to hit that particular spot on earth, my father would be safely seated in the car. She tripped and fell before we even realized what had happened. We always concentrate on our father; my mother is never the object of worry, although she is a very sick person. That's how she trained us.

My heart stopped. I prayed she hadn't broken her hip. I ran to the trunk, deposited their stuff, and ran back to my mother. She was groaning, and I couldn't gage the extent of the damage. Alex seated my father in the car and ran back to help me. We literally had to carry her to the car. We offered to take them back home, but my mom insisted that she was not hurt too badly.

"Is this some kind of joke?" my father exclaimed. "She's my guide, and now she's falling? How do you expect me to walk now? I'm the one who can fall, not her! What irony!"

I was very upset with him and started, "Papa—"

But Alex didn't let me finish. He feverishly stomped on my foot, which was my cue to shut up.

I quickly changed my sentence. "Papa, are you comfortable there?"

We made quite an entrance when we finally arrived at Greg's.

"My most important guests are here!" Greg cried. "Mama, what happened?"

"Vika, I couldn't put the mozzarella on the table. I've been waiting for the beef tomatoes," Nelly blurted without so much as a hello.

Oh my God, I had completely forgotten that I forgot to bring tomatoes! Could I blame it on my mom's accident? Probably not…

My father was almost hysterically laughing. "How do you like this? She's my guide dog. I always hold onto her arm because I'm the one who is likely to fall and who is *really* ailing, not her! So what will we all do now that I have no support?"

My mom went directly to the sofa and propped up her leg.

Greg ran to get her an ice pack and said, "Papa, we've told you a million times that you have to start walking with the walker. It's hard for mom to carry you because you put your entire weight on her. She is old, too."

"They will never see me walking with the walker—never!"

"Who's *they*?"

"My friends, neighbors, anybody. My old friend, Benjamin, is the same age as me, and he's still running. I can imagine how happy he'll be to see me so fragile and weak. They'll all be happy."

"Papa," Greg said, "Benjamin's only son was killed in a car accident last year. I don't think he cares too much that he walks straight and you don't. He would gladly switch places with you—or even with his son."

"Oh, don't give me this crap! Everybody is selfish and cares only about himself. I'm sure he *will* be happy that he walks, while I crawl with a walker."

He clearly didn't understand the point Greg was trying to make. If my father had to go through what Benjamin went through and lose me, he would say, "Why is life so unfair? Why couldn't she die the day after I died so that I wouldn't have to be so upset?"

I ran to the kitchen to help Nelly. I put the salads I had prepared on the table and the mashed potatoes in the microwave. I confessed that I had forgotten the tomatoes and called myself such horrible names that Nelly was left with none. She said I needn't be so hard on myself; it was just tomatoes, after all.

We all sat around the table at our usual places. It felt so wonderful; we were *the* family. A couple of friends joined us, and Danny came later, when we were all sitting around the table. Everybody was admiring him, I could tell. He never cared about fancy clothes, but whatever he wore was always very neat and looked good on his lean and muscular body. And he was unfailingly funny, informative, and brilliant. Alex frequently commented on his handsome appearance. He made his rounds, kissing every family member but me. At last, he shook hands with Alex and went to sit at his usual place.

Did they notice that he hadn't even said hi to me? I'm sure they didn't.

Alex squeezed my knee under the table as a way of saying, "I know, I know."

My mom momentarily forgot she was injured and jumped to get all available food for Danny, which aggravated him and Nelly immensely. Nelly would give Greg a hard time afterward because his mom paid more attention to Danny than to their children. The fact that Danny didn't always have food, unlike her children, was of no importance—fair is fair.

My sensitive brother took notice of what had just happened—or rather, what had not happened—between Danny and me. Thus, he decided to alter the usual routine. "Let's raise a toast to Vika since we missed her birthday this year. She is a wonderful daughter, sister, mother, and wife. I am sure her parents, son, and husband will agree with me. Danny, your speech, please."

Danny looked annoyed by this, but Greg was always a no-nonsense uncle with him. Danny raised a glass of water (he never drank), and said, "Mother, to you. You are the best mother I've ever had."

Everybody laughed, and I breathed a sigh of relief. He came to me and hugged me. I couldn't ask for a better belated birthday gift, could I?

Now we could return to our ritual.

Our first toast is always "God Bless America," which is supremely uncool and makes many people grimace, I know. If you could only know how strongly we feel about it. But what do you know? You have never experienced anything different; you don't think too much of living the way you do. All right, all right, enough propaganda.

We had gotten through the salads and appetizers. My dad asked my mom, "Rachel, did you try this fish? Will *I* eat it?"

Finally came the moment of truth. Nelly went to the kitchen to retrieve the guest of honor. Greg ran to grab the camera; all guests were summoned from outside to witness the grand entrance. And then she entered the dining room dressed like a bride, with her radiant golden skin and a bright-red bow on her very short neck (I do hope you realize I'm not talking about Nelly), atop an ornate platter and surrounded by all kinds of fruit and berries. We all gaped in awe at this sight to behold and screamed a big *wow*! We would scream it in any event; you would too if you knew Nelly. But this unanimous "wow" was very well deserved. Nobody made turkey like our Nelly—nobody. My mother, Nelly's mother-in-law, said just that: "Nobody makes turkey like our Nelly—nobody."

Another special aspect of Nelly's turkey was the extra dark meat she added to the tray. We all liked dark meat, and there were never enough legs and thighs to go around. So, for years,

Nelly bought extra pieces, just the legs, and cooked them with the whole turkey. The turkey, as a result, looked like a very nicely dressed Shiva with ten legs. Greg took tons of pictures from every possible angle—Nelly entering the room with the turkey, Nelly putting the turkey on the table, and Nelly making the first cut. They both were so well dressed and well fed.

Nelly sliced the bird, and we subsequently began our annual ritual of moaning profusely while eating this special turkey that only our Nelly could master. We laughed, ate, drank, and enjoyed the evening of this wonderful, wonderful holiday.

My mom, who was not even listening to our conversations (which happened with her all the time lately), all of a sudden said, "Nelly, dear, I have not seen Sofia for a long time. How is she? I was sure I would see her here tonight."

My dearest mommy—that was the second time that day she made my heart stop. If only I hadn't run into Sofia earlier that morning I would be as happy a camper as everybody else around the table.

"We invited them, of course," Greg assured her, "but they said they had promised somebody else a long time ago. I'm a little offended, to be honest. We waited for them for so long, we put so much effort into bringing them here, and now we hardly see them. Even for the kids' sake, Sofia should have come tonight. Our kids are the only cousins they have. Why not give them the opportunity to grow closer? Her kids could learn so much from ours, who are real Americans. I know Nelly is very hurt by it. But, on the other hand, they are newcomers, and it's probably easier for them to hang out with others of their own stature. Also, maybe jealousy plays some role in this, too."

Had he rehearsed this speech with Nelly? My Greg is too decent to say such things.

"People!" Nelly chimed in. "It would be ironic if she came tonight. Thanksgiving is about giving thanks. When I remember how much time I spent preparing all the papers it took to apply for their coming."

"Greg, I can't remember, who applied for you when you came here?" I asked.

"Our neighbors' children."

"Where are they now?"

Alex kicked my leg under the table—and not flirtatiously. He was giving me a warning to shut up again. If I had went to the police the next day and showed them my legs, he would have gone to prison for domestic violence!

Nelly, annoyed by my interruption, retorted, "How do we know? Somewhere. Who cares? Anyway, I never imagined that it would turn out this way. She's probably upset that we are well off, living in a nice house and driving nice cars. What did she expect? They have to go through everything we went through to get what we have. I gave her ten thousand dollars that my parents left! And she looked upset! Ten thousand dollars! Isn't that good money for someone who just got here? Nobody gave me ten thousand dollars when I came here! I could have used it, too! My parents left the money to their grandchildren. Sofia's son and daughter both got accepted to UCLA. That's the kind of education they still have in Russia. They come here, and only two years later, both of them are in UCLA! Try getting your kids accepted by UCLA! Oh yea, your Danny got in there, too. All kids who come here from Russia have such drive that nothing can stop them," Nelly accused.

Alex and I exchanged laughing glances.

She continued, "My kids weren't accepted there. And guess what? We had to send them to expensive private schools. She cannot even imagine how much we are paying a year for the two tuitions. She had a free ride! UCLA is a bargain compared to our kids' colleges. So she saved tens of thousands—if not hundreds—of dollars right there. And now she is barely talking to me? If my parents knew how much I have to pay for my children compared to hers, they would have left all the money to my children. I'm fine, and I don't need their money, but my children might. They don't have that kind of drive or even that kind of brain, so they need more support. Weaker people need more support. Isn't that common knowledge?"

She wound herself into this rage to prove to herself that she was right.

The room became extremely quiet.

A minute later, she added, "Ten thousand dollars is not good enough money for her. She is ready to lose her sister over this lousy ten thousand dollars. And who was here taking care of her parents while she was still in Russia?" She couldn't get over it.

"Nelly, that's not fair," Greg refuted. "They were your parents, too. And she would have been happy to be here with them, but they were trapped there. Your parents helped a lot with those papers, and they paid for all of that."

"That's my husband! Are you on my side or hers?"

"You know I'm always on your side."

He'd better be. The silence had, ones again, fallen over the room.

My dad broke it. "Yes, life has some twists. Can you believe that I was the unstable one and she was the one holding me, and now she starts to fall? Now what?"

~

PART 3

I LOVE MY LIFE

CHAPTER 19
ALEX'S FIFTIETH BIRTHDAY

We were married for eight years when Alex's very big birthday was approaching. As you know, he doesn't like celebrations of any kind. He absolutely despises the publicity and attention, which is the reason why we never celebrated anything. We would go out of town for the weekend to celebrate our birthdays or anniversaries, just the two of us.

But this was not just another birthday. I suggested we do something special. He was very adamant about his decision. He declared that we would go to Las Vegas and get as wild and extravagant as his strict discipline, his lack of excitement, and the worsening financial situation in the country would allow us. And so we did. And we did have a very good time. We even "accidentally" ran into our friends—the couple I secretly called the week before to say that we would be there. But I felt that I couldn't let his fiftieth birthday slip through my fingers. This grand event necessitated action.

So before we left for Las Vegas, I reserved a private room at a very nice Italian restaurant for the Saturday after our trip and invited forty-plus people (not counting family) to attend a surprise party to celebrate Alex's fiftieth birthday. I added that there would be no hard feelings if anybody couldn't make it. To my surprise, every single person confirmed that he or she was coming. So there was no going back. Honestly, I was freaking out. I was terrified that Alex would be furious with me. I wasn't even sure if acting against his will was ethical. But I wanted so badly to do something for him that I decided it would be a semi-surprise party. I established that we would have to go out one more time to appease our immediate family: his sister, Kathy (who was visiting from New York because I told her about my secret plan); my brother and his family; Julia and Danny, with their significant (at the time) others; and my parents. So he expected there would be thirteen of us. At least he was ready for thirteen. I comforted myself in knowing that if he was amenable to thirteen, he might as well not mind another forty. I, again, took chances, as I always do. Nelly calls me "wild Vika," suggesting that even she cannot always control me, and controlling everybody and everything is her self-imposed purpose in life.

When we came back from Las Vegas, I had a whole week to throw a perfect birthday party for my perfect husband. I enjoyed every minute of the preparations. Alex couldn't believe my sudden cleaning fit; usually, he's the one who does almost all the work around the house. I planned to return to our place after the restaurant for coffee, tea, desserts, more drinking, and entertainment, so I decorated the house accordingly and ordered a huge cake worthy of a world cake contest—that's how beautiful and tasty it was. I put three folding tables next to our usual two tables, and Alex was clueless as to why we needed so many tables if only thirteen people were coming over after dinner to have some tea. But if a woman needs fabricate a story, no man can outsmart her. I exaggerated that I needed one table just to put a cake and candles on and the second to put all the glasses and plates on so that I wouldn't be running around while all the guests were there.

That Saturday, I drove a rather long distance to pick up *the* cake. When I came home with it, he asked why the box was so humongous. I cleverly said that they didn't have a smaller box, so they put my small cake in a big box to protect it from being damaged during my drive. Little did he know...

The closer we were to the time to go to the restaurant, the more nervous I became. I remembered our dear friend Monie's surprise party, and I was afraid my party would end the same way. If you have not heard what happened at poor Monie's birthday, I will tell you now.

As Monica Lisa's, or "Monie" as we all call her, big birthday was approaching, she told her husband, Sigismund, that she was feeling depressed and didn't want a big celebration. They went to Las Vegas for a few days, just as we did. On Friday night, the day of her birthday, they were coming back. But Sigismund would not be Sigismund if he let it pass by like that. If you think I'm unruly, you would think again if you met Sigismund. He wants to experience everything in life to the extreme, and more often than not, it ends dramatically—to say the least. So he decided to do it his way again. He called us all and said that he was throwing a surprise party for Monie and asked if we wanted to participate. Of course, we all wanted to celebrate our beloved Monie's big birthday.

"All right," said Sigismund, "since we have to go to Las Vegas, I physically will be in Las Vegas, but will be supervising everything via cell phone, and you guys will only have to do the rest."

Translated to plain language, this meant we had to do everything, and he would just give us the keys to their house and bring Monie home on time. Only Sigismund could get away with it because we all loved him dearly. He would do the same and more for anybody, even if that anybody didn't want it. That's our dangerous Sigismund.

Well, we all shared the responsibilities—some cooking, some buying liquor, some decorating the house, and some setting the tables in the huge living room. I got away easy this time; I wrote a funny song about both of them that I planned to sing with the girls. I do this very rarely—only for very special people.

Sigismund was scheduled to bring Monie to their place by 7:00 p.m. We all gathered there by 5:30 p.m. to get ready. There were thirty-some people; everybody parked on other streets and walked there so Monie wouldn't suspect anything when they arrived at the house and would enjoy the surprise to the fullest.

Their children and young grandchildren all came dressed up, bringing lavish gifts and extravagant flower arrangements. We brought our boxes of gifts, too, and everything was situated in the middle of the family room. We had no more than four video cameras and four still cameras at the ready. All suggested that Sigismund planned for the surprise to be fully televised. All thirty of us crammed into the medium-sized family room, where we were stepping on each other's toes and nerves. Two little girls were very excited to be dressed as princesses and carry flowers, and a little baby boy was crawling around, and we were trying hard not to trample him.

One of the guys who was Sigismund's appointee recited what we had to do and in what order to make the party a huge success—according to Sigismund's definition of success, of course. I think some notorious husband who planned to lawfully kill his wife in order to collect her inheritance invented the surprise party many years ago. So I always wonder what the definition of a successful surprise party really was.

An hour passed, and we regrouped. One of us was supposed to turn the lights on when the door opened; others were supposed to scream their lungs out with "Surprise!" The media guys were supposed to catch the shock on poor

Monie's face, the little girls' assignment was to run ahead with the flowers, and the baby boy's assignment was to not get killed. You would think that his parents were supposed to be watching after him, but in America, it's usually the father who takes care of the babies—don't ask me why. But the father was busy with the cameras.

The closer it got to 7:00 p.m., the more nervous we became. Sigismund called a few times from the car and gave us their coordinates in cryptic messages. By 7:45, we were very hungry, very thirsty, and very anxious. About ten times somebody yelled that they were coming, and we would turn off the lights and start yelling at each other to shut up. The women yelled at the men that they didn't know how speak in a whisper. The men shot back that the women didn't talk loudly because, every time the lights went down, they snuck to the living room to steal food.

Finally, Sigismund called the appointee's cell again and said, "Is this the Home Depot? Sorry, wrong number."

We turned the lights off again, and soon we could hear the garage door opening.

The lady who was supposed to turn the lights on as soon as Monie entered the room couldn't hold it anymore, and two minutes before they arrived, she ran to use the bathroom. She asked the lady next to her to turn on the lights in case they came. When the door from the garage to the family room opened, and we could see poor Monie standing by the door, we all jumped from our seats and screamed, "Surprise!" But the other lady who had just become responsible for turning on the lights did not practice it before and couldn't find the switch in the dark. Camera flashes began illuminating the dark room, capturing shots of poor Monie with a look of complete horror on her face. We couldn't understand why the lights were still off. The little girls tried to run ahead as planned to meet their grandma with the beautiful roses, but since it was absolutely dark and the flashes blinded them, they tripped over the pile of packages in the middle of the room, falling on the gifts and the roses. The rose thorns pricked one of the four little arms, and they both started screaming hysterically, even the one who wasn't hurt. Greg decided to end this disaster and at least find the switch to turn on the lights. He accidentally pushed the grandfather clock, and they both fell, barely missing the baby boy. The baby got so spooked by everybody jumping and screaming in complete darkness that he began crying hysterically, and his parents couldn't calm him down for the rest of the evening.

But all of this was nothing compared to what happened to our birthday girl. After five hours of driving, Monie was very tired and planned to take it easy. They lived alone; therefore, the house should have been empty upon their arrival. But when she opened the door, she could hear the toilet flushing. Then, in the complete darkness, she saw some shades jump, something flashed, somebody screamed, and what happened after that she would never know because she dropped dead.

When somebody finally found the light switch, we could see the damage. We saw that poor Monie had dropped in a dead faint on the floor. She was carrying pillows from the car when she entered, but unfortunately, she and the pillows dropped in different directions. Sigismund the monster was standing in the doorway behind her, not understanding what in his perfect plan had gone so wrong. The good news was that he's a doctor. The thing about doctors, though, is that they have no mercy—at least it always appears that way. He was at once calm and annoyed with her and with us. In a matter-of-fact manner, he started to bark out orders on how to carry Monie to the sofa, how to hold her head, and what to do with the girls and the baby. He sat by Monie and started to revive her. Ten times we tried to call 911, but he wouldn't let us; he said it would be too hard to explain to them what had happened. He was willing to sacrifice his beloved wife to his ambitions.

In time, Monie opened her eyes. Sigismund gave her heart medication and a sedative and announced that she was ready to celebrate. We wildly protested this crazy idea, but he insisted that they were both very hungry because he hadn't let her eat all day knowing that they would have a very nice spread waiting for them at home. He explained that her hunger probably contributed to her fatigue. I doubt it very much, but to think that he didn't allow her to eat on her birthday to make this surprise even wilder made me very angry. You have to *adore* your husband—which she obviously does and it's mutual—to take such abuse.

So we all trudged into the living room, decorated with all the stupid balloons, cards, and toys we had brought. Sigismund dragged poor Monie and seated her at the head of the table. She could not stop crying, no matter how hard she tried to smile. Everyone was overwhelmed with guilt. Sigismund told us not to worry. He gave her another sedative, put some ice on her swelling arm, and the party began. The first toast was his, of course. For a good ten minutes, he stated how much he loved her and how special she was, as if we weren't already aware. Just imagine how she agreed to continually endure all his crazy projects. Then, one by one, we all said our toasts, followed by much needed drinks. My turn came, and I was supposed to sing my stupid funny song. It was just as well that it was supposed to be a surprise for both of them, so he didn't know about it, and I could skip it without consequence. If I had to sing it, I would have started crying, no doubt about it.

Then it was poor Monie's turn to give her speech. She said that she was very overwhelmed by the love and attention of her husband and friends and that she was so touched by it that she wanted to cry. And, at that, she started weeping uncontrollably. Sigismund gave her more wine and prompted her to open and admire all her gifts—or whatever was left of them. The physical damage was limited to one little cut arm, Monie's bruises from falling down (which became more noticeable the next day), one Limoges jewelry box (a gift from the children), Greg's eyeglasses (which he lost when he fell and were stepped on in the dark), and a broken antique grandfather clock. Not a big deal. But the damage to the psyche…

Oh well, Sigismund gave more sedatives to poor Monie—and I suspect even some to the still-screaming baby—and minimized the emotional damage. Poor Monie looked like a zombie but tried hard to smile and indicate that she was very pleased. She mastered a very faint and mysterious Minie Lisa Shapiro smile. We only hoped that he would not give her an overdose.

This is the story of that really successful surprise party. No one could deny that she was *truly* surprised. So the mission was accomplished.

Now you can understand why I was paranoid about having a too successful surprise party. But, as I said, it was going to be a semi-surprise party. Plus, it wouldn't be completely dark at the restaurant, so I hoped it wouldn't turn out quite like that.

When we entered the restaurant, and Alex saw all the people there, and they all screamed, "Surprise!" he was very startled. And then he started laughing, and then, unfortunately, he started crying. What is it with all these birthday people? Why do they always have to do that to you? But at least I could see that his were happy tears. I could see that he was very emotional, but he was not angry with me.

"I knew my wife was crazy," Alex quipped, "but I didn't realize to what extent."

The only person who arrived after us was Julia. She made her entrance when everybody was already eating, and she looked as spectacular as always. Alex was so pleased to see how everybody jumped to greet her and pay her all due compliments.

We had a wonderful dinner at the restaurant, and then everyone went to our place for dessert. The beautiful cake was brought out, and we sang "Happy Birthday" to Alex. Then the girls stayed in the dining room with the cake and tea, and the boys collected in the kitchen with the tequila and every possible appetizer I could find in the fridge. (We had just eaten, right?)

As the evening wore on, all the guests appeared to be enjoying themselves, so I gathered everyone into the living room and announced that I had prepared some entertainment. I had written a humorous song to share in honor of Alex's birthday celebration. It was one of my numerous hobbies. Alex enthusiastically supported all of them. Whether I was knitting, beading, painting, or writing short stories, he was proud of anything I did and praised me for it. When such a *mensch*[1] admires you, it makes you feel much better about yourself.

As I mentioned before, I only write songs for very important occasions, and this was the most momentous of them all. Maggie accompanied me on our piano keyboard as I sang. You cannot appreciate the lyrics, of course, because they were in Russian. But, believe me, it was funny. And then I read a poem I had written as well. I never write serious poems, only humorous ones. And, in everyday life, we usually joke because it helps you make it through the day. But it was not your everyday day; it was a special event. I meant every word of the lines written below:

WHAT IS LOVE?

Can anybody tell me what love is?

---

1   A person of integrity and honor (Yiddish)

Not only serenades and lust submission,
Not gifts, not flattery, not that, not this.
What is it then? Please, give me the definition.

Or maybe love is just a word, and therefore,
It has no meaning. It's invented for survival.
It's easier to pay your mortgages, you know,
If someone's helping your financial revival.

Someone will tell you that it's all of the above.
Another will reply with yet another answer,
Like lover has to fit his suit like glove,
Or to impress your friends by being a good dancer.

But as for me…let's say you have it all—
A job, a car, a house, and a fortune—
You have succeeded, you're standing tall,
But something's missing and you feel like an orphan.

So if you ask me what I need in life,
I need my son be happy and my parents healthy,
My books, my job, my friends, some luck.
And if I have all that, then I'm already wealthy.

But what I need to breathe, to smell, to shine;
To feel unique, exquisite, brilliant,
And to be seen as special person I'm not
But always dreamt to be and never will be.

Someone who tolerates my mishigases²,
Who finds all my achievements great and failures cute,

---

2   Yiddish for craziness

My friend, my mate, my confidant, my buddy,
Then what I need for all of that is You.

I saw tears in Alex's eyes, and he came over to kiss me. What a kisser he was! But I couldn't write about that, could I? He looked so happy with so many loving people around him, with Julia sitting there looking so beautiful, and with me who did it all to make him happy. His eyes sparkled—our bright chandelier and the tears in his eyes contributed to it a lot.

For the next week or two, Alex called anyone and everyone in the world to tell them what a grandiose surprise party his Vika had thrown for him. "Hey, old man," he would say, "you will not believe what my crazy Vika put me through!" And he would go on and on, half complaining and half bragging about it, and the words *my Vika* were used to begin every sentence: "My Vika said…My Vika sang…My Vika brought a huge cake and lied to me that it was a small cake for eight people and only the box was huge…"

I had asked Danny to take pictures throughout the night, and later on, when he uploaded them, it turned out to be the most beautiful album. He did a superb job, as any job my Danny does. Later, I secretly ordered a big eighteen-month wall calendar with those pictures as the focus. And, a couple of weeks later, when Alex opened the mail and saw the calendar with the picture of him on the cover, he started crying all over again and got very surprised all over again and loved me all over again.

Oh Alex, my Alex.

Oh, those memorable little things! How important they are! The most important, I would say. If only we could be left alone with each other, how we would enjoy life! We always thought we knew how to do it better than anybody else.

❧

CHAPTER 20
QUIET LIFE

Sometimes we really missed each other because we worked too much and had too little free time to spend together. So when our schedules finally coincided, we wanted to be together, just the two of us. We never tired of each other, even though it had been ten years since we first met!

It was Alex's rule that I had to sit next to him to watch the nightly news at 10:00. Sometimes I wanted to cheat and skip it, but he was very strict about it. We had to face all that horror together.

He was inexorably obsessed with the weather, probably because he often worked outside. The way they gradually unveil the forecast for the next day's weather is fascinating. It's like an Agatha Christie mystery. The attractive newscaster lures you to stay tuned with comments like, "You will not believe what's in store for us over the next twenty-four hours in regard to the upcoming weather. Are you ready for a big surprise? Well, we'll have the complete forecast for you coming up next." Then they report a few murders and air a few commercials, which usually tell you where to get a bigger and juicier burger or how to lose weight. Alex, having to wake up at 5:30 a.m., would love to go to sleep right there, but he was hooked! Something was cooking over there at the news station at 10:00—some conspiracy about weather! What if he doesn't even have to wake up at 5:30 anymore? What if we all won't wake up anymore? So he remains firmly ensconced in his position on the couch. Ten minutes later, that pretty, secretive girl would continue unfolding the mystery.

"Here's what you can expect over the next twenty-four hours. Let's take a look at what the radar map is showing us. We prepared this fragment exclusively for you."

Did she mean Alex only, or was I included as well? She is very eye-catching. Should I start worrying?

She went on, "We are expecting a big storm—almost a hurricane. Will it hit our shores? Stay tuned to find out."

Women. She was definitely flirting with Alex, so he was even more deeply hooked by now. We stayed awake for a few more murders, and then, finally, she had mercy. She turned to the very high-tech map so that Alex could see her curvaceous body in profile, complete with a flat stomach, big breasts, and a very high butt. (How do they do that on television?)

"Here are the two vectors showing how this monstrous storm will move. If high pressure develops in this area here, we will see this devastating storm reach our shores. But if high pressure develops in this area right here, the storm will go to Northern California and Oregon. What we know for sure at this point in time is that we either have a storm tomorrow or not. But we will keep a very close eye on it, and tomorrow we will report to you what happened . But, just in case, have your umbrellas handy."

Alex always carried a heavy-duty umbrella in his van anyway. So he would turn off the TV and go to sleep. The next evening, they would play the same game again.

On Saturdays, he usually worked, but on Sundays, we always went to the beach. We spent all day there, walking along the ocean, going out to lunch, going to the movies, having dinner, and driving home in the evening. On the drive home, he would put his hand on my shoulder, and I would say again, "I love my life."

Life was good.

Sometimes we met up with Julia and spent Sundays together. She was getting older and, with that, more reasonable. When she was not "warm" on something, she was quite pleasant; I was somewhat getting along with her again, as long as we stayed with small talk.

I remember one funny conversation we shared. We were sitting at some oceanside café having lunch and talking about her new job and her old friends.

"You, Vika," she iterated, "are always praising this country. Helloooo, they don't care about us little guys! But you wouldn't know."

"Julia, it doesn't go by weight, but by significance. So I would know; I'm a small guy, too. And so is your dad, even though he's a little taller than average."

"No, you're not part of it. You've been working all of your life, so of course, you're better off. Do you know that they only talk about how we support disabled people in this country? But when it comes to like the real test...I know this girl who was on drugs before, but now she's fine and some government agency found her a job. They sent her to some school first, and then she started working as a school bus driver. In a few weeks, she was laid off! And you know the reason they gave her? That she is like too fat and her stomach doesn't let her turn the wheel! It's a disease when a person is *that* fat. What is she supposed to do if she's sick? So she can't turn the wheel? Big deal! Talk about discrimination!"

"Julia, with all due respect to you, to her, and to the government agencies, I never saw people that fat back in Russia—never ever, not even once. Do you suppose they're all healthy there? Or, say, in Africa? If you cannot work because you're too fat, you have to go out of your way to lose weight. The same applies when you're on drugs. It's your problem, not the government's."

"Easy to say. You yourself gained a good twenty pounds in the last few years. Is it easy to lose it? Is it?"

"Yep, you're right. I gained seventeen pounds."

"So are you happy about it? Especially having a gorgeous husband like my father?"

She caught me off guard; I never expected any kind of logical thinking from her. "Julia, I'm so glad you pointed that all out."

I probably should be very thankful to her. I lost my mind—that's how angry it made me with myself. Of course, I shouldn't lecture about self-discipline if I myself became a pig.

I enrolled in Weight Watchers and made losing weight a top priority. It took me around six months to look nicer and twelve months to look really nice. Maybe not nice nice, but as nice as I looked seventeen pounds ago, when Alex didn't fall in love with me at first sight.

Thanks, Julia!

CHAPTER 21
CHAIN E-MAILS

"Did you read my e-mail? Do you ever open your e-mails?" Belka chastised me the moment I answered the phone.

We usually talked on the phone and rarely e-mailed each other, as we were both overwhelmed with e-mails and hated it—especially chain e-mails. Don't get me started on that subject.

"Why did you e-mail me? Can't you call?"

"You will not believe what a nasty and stupid e-mail I received from my very dear and very dumb friend Irina."

"Belka, we've talked about this a million times. Just delete it. If these people who forward garbage to all the people they know had to pay one cent of postage for it, they would think twice. So what if she sent you another syrupy e-mail about friendship or love or what a very special and unique person you—and the other two hundred of her correspondents—are."

"No! This time she forwarded me such a nasty thing I want to cry, or laugh, or both. This time it's about how good sex is for you, your heart, stomach, liver, hair, and all other organs! But that's not all! At the end there is this threat."

She read the following passage to me over the phone:

This message has been sent to you for good luck in sex. The original is in a room in the basement of the Dwight House Pub. It has been sent around the world nine times. Now sex has been sent to you. The "Hot Sex Fairy" will visit you within four days of receiving this message, provided you, in turn, send it on.

If you don't, then you will never receive good sex again for the rest of your life. You will eventually become celibate, and your genitals will rot and fall off. This is no joke! Send copies to people you think need sex (who doesn't?). Don't send money, as the fate of your genitals has no price. Do not keep this message. This message must leave your inbox in five hours. Please send ten copies and see what happens in four days.[3]

"I want to kill her!" she continued, exasperated. "I cannot send it to anybody who I call a friend, and I know it's all BS, but it's so disturbing! Read it all. You will not believe your eyes. I just sent it to you."

"You sent it to me? Didn't you just say you couldn't forward it to anybody who you call a friend?"

"I didn't forward it to you with the intention of passing this threat to you. I just wanted to show you how far these things can go."

"Do you suppose the Sex Fairy will know your intentions? And now what? I have to wait to see if my genitals rot and fall off? Just wait until I show this message to Alex! He will send it back to you and your idiot Irina one hundred times. Oh, wait a minute, if my computer was bought with the money from our joint account, does that mean Alex's genitals will fall off as well?"

"Vika, you don't really believe this crap, do you?"

"No, I don't. But to send threats like that? All these stupid, nauseating e-mails are being created by some college or high school boys who are having fun watching it spread around like wildfire by stupid housewives who happen to know

---

3   This e-mail is really circulating (author)

where to click to open e-mail. Chain e-mails are weapons of mass destruction."

"You know what? Let's create one."

"Do I look like a college boy to you?"

"Maybe a little in your upper body…You never were famous for your breasts."

"Look who's talking. All right, let's do it. I'll compose it and send it to you in five minutes."

I collected all my intelligence and wrote a very benign and average chain e-mail. I sent it to Belka and called her.

"Did you get it?"

"I got it. Did you really just make that up? You're a genius! It's as sentimental and senseless as it gets."

"Thanks a lot. I love you, too. Now, I am not sure about the usual threat at the end. How severe do you want it to be?"

"I told you the people you're planning to send it to are your friends, not enemies."

"Very well then, here is the ending. I will send you the whole opus, and you decide whom you want to send it to. Call me when it goes around the world nine times and comes back to you."

The following is what I sent her, and she started the thread:

Seven is a lucky number. Write it down on paper, chew and swallow it, and you will touch eternity.

Seven rules to follow:

1. *When you wake up, think of hungry children in Africa, and you will feel better about your obesity. Then go back to sleep.*

2. *Listen to a storm and hurricane recording, and you will feel blessed to spend twelve hours every day in the office, providing the ceiling is not leaking.*

3. *Don't take your job too seriously; let other people (or welfare) take care of you.*

4. *Don't take anybody too seriously; they don't take you seriously, either.*
5. *Try to like your boss; he's a human, too…maybe.*
6. *Put a flower under your pillow, and an angel will visit you.*
7. *If you don't feel like cleaning your room, don't feel bad; there's a lot of mess in the world.*
   Pass this on to those who you love or hate or don't care about, and you will all form a fraternity.

Oh God, do I hate chain e-mails!

Two months later, in the middle of huge turmoil, when I absolutely forgot about all this, Belka called.

"Vika, I have news! I received our chain e-mail back—the one we started! It came from my school friend, and she lives in Australia now! You are currently popular around the world! Just one thing—they changed our mild ending to something quite threatening. I would say they broke our copyright."

CHAPTER 22
ALEX'S COUSIN COMES TO VISIT

Alex was a consummate family man. It was very unfortunate for him that his first marriage did not work. And even though it always takes two to ruin it, in his case, it took one, and it was by no means his fault. Nevertheless, he was unceasingly nostalgic about family ties.

With that said, I was not surprised when he told me that he wanted to invite his only cousin from Russia to visit. And since that cousin of his was not the rich New Russian but the poor Old Jew (just joking, he was Alex's age), we had to pay for everything, which was plenty. I tried to reason with him against this idea. But when it came to his family, Alex was adamant. He was very nostalgic for his late mother, who died before her time (younger than we were then), and I think he was subconsciously trying to reconnect with her in any way he could.

So the cousin was coming. His name was…Alex. Actually, their name was Alexander; it is a very popular name in Russia. When my Alex came here, he shortened it and became Alex. But I still cannot understand how it could happen that, in the same family, two sisters would name their sons of the same age the same name. They probably were not on speaking terms at the time.

For the sake of the story, I will call our Russian guest Alexander. I had experienced my share of two Alexes already. Oh, wait a minute! You did not hear my story of the two Alexes yet! Now is the time.

I had to stay late at the office because I was on call, and there was a problem at a customer's site. Being alone and under big pressure, I decided to call the girl whose product was misbehaving. She was a young Russian girl named Stella. We were very close friends. Her husband's name was Alex as well. I picked up the phone and pushed the button for placed calls to quickly find her number in the list. I knew it started with our area code and ended with 65, so I found the corresponding number in the call log and pushed redial. As it happens, my Alex's cell phone number also starts with the same area code and ends with 65. Of all the numbers, I accidentally picked my Alex's cell, and he was taking a nap while waiting for me to come home. Believe it or not, cell phones alter a person's voice. Plus, he was almost whispering. As a result, I swear I did not recognize my Alex's voice and was sure I was talking to Stella's Alex. Here is how it went:

"Alex, good evening. This is Victoria," I said.

"No shit," he said.

If I had not been under such stress, that response would have alarmed me right there. But my lively imagination always helps in stressful situations. I remembered that they had a close friend of their age whose name was Victoria, too. Their children were friends, and they spent a lot of time carpooling, sleeping over, and the like. I concluded Stella's Alex had mistaken me with the other Victoria, which might have explained why he was talking to me with such familiarity, so I went on.

"I'm sorry to bother you. You're probably about to sit down to dinner."

"I would be if you cooked something for us."

Now I was positive that he had taken me for the other Vika if he joked like that. Oh well, who cared? I needed Stella.

"You know, I'm still at work," I continued.

"I figured."

"I have a crisis here. I really need to talk to Stella."

"Then talk to her! Do you need my permission? OK, you have my permission."

I paused and then said, "So…"

"So what do you want from me?"

"Can you call Stella for me, please?" I was becoming slightly irritated.

"I call Stella?" he responded. "You call her if you need her."

"Is Stella there?"

"Is Stella here? Do you mean that young, pretty girl from your office? I wish…Vika, are you sure you know where you're calling?" he started to yell.

And, just then, I knew!

"Alex, is that you? It was you the whole time? I have such a crisis here! Why didn't you tell me right away that you weren't Alex and not waste my time?"

"Tell you that I'm not Alex?"

The line went dead. The nerve of him!

The next morning, I went to the office and told Stella what had happened the night before. She laughed like crazy. Later that day, when we had our group meeting, Stella told everybody that I had a hilarious story to tell. I recounted the whole story, adding a few unimportant, yet funny details, and everybody laughed like crazy, too. At a department meeting later in the week, my manager announced to the group that I had a humorous story of the two Alexes to share. I insisted everybody had heard the story already, but some of them alleged they had not. I, therefore, had no choice but to retell the story. As expected, they laughed hysterically. My manager even

AFTER THE HAPPY END

attested that every time she heard the story it had more and more amusing details and that every time she liked it even more.

Dressed in our best evening attire, we were all enjoying ourselves at our company's annual Christmas party a month later when, suddenly, my boss said, "My husband never heard the story of the two Alexes."

"No way. We have all heard it a million times."

The other spouses, including mine, said that they wanted to hear it, too. I feared Alex would not recognize the original story. Even I couldn't recall what was authentic and what was not. So I continued to play modest and shy. But they cajoled me into telling the story of the two Alexes once again. They, of course, all delighted in the tale, including my Alex. He laughed so hard.

"Is that really how it was?" my boss asked him.

"Yes, of course," he said

That's my Alex. He will never let me down; I am so safe with him—always.

Back to Alexander. We bought him an airline ticket and medical insurance, booked hotels in Las Vegas and Santa Barbara, and prepared for his arrival in mid-November.

In the weeks prior to his visit, we readied ourselves to celebrate Halloween. Alex adores Halloween. He always goes to the Russian store, buys a bucket of expensive Russian chocolates, dons some costume, sits by the door, and waits for trick-or-treaters. He doesn't just hand out candy; he converses with the kids in his broken English, asking them to explain their costumes or making them dance and sing before doling out plenty of chocolates. Sometimes, however, little kids don't understand what he wants from them. I don't take pleasure in this ritual and never participate.

134

This particular year was no different. The only difference that evening was he also cleaned out our pantry in anticipation of his cousin's arrival, throwing away open bottles of wine. I told you before that we don't drink, so every time somebody comes to visit and we open a bottle, it remains untouched until we throw it away. But this time, for some unknown reason, he became thrifty. He complained that some wine was exquisite and regretted buying it and not drinking it and so on. Having just come home from work and wanting to take a shower, I paid no attention to any of his exploits, as I wanted no part of this Halloween extravaganza; I simply don't understand a holiday celebrating the dead.

When I entered our kitchen, Alex was in the middle of a telephone conversation. I noticed a few glasses full of wine on the counter, and I saw him downing one of them—apparently, not his first one. I could not believe my eyes. Then I turned my attention to his exchange. As you realize, I could only hear his side of the conversation.

"What did you say your name was? Annette?" Alex asked.

The person on the other end of the line said something back.

"My cousin? Wait a minute. My Aunty Berta's daughter? Who is Aunty Berta?"

The caller attempted to provide further clarification.

"I'm sorry, I don't remember. Oh, she was not my aunt but my Uncle Boris's first wife? Twice removed? Who was twice removed—the first wife? Oh, he was my uncle twice removed? Aha, I think I am getting it," Alex said agonizingly, but I could clearly see that he was not getting it. He covered the receiver with his hand and said to me, "My close relative is calling. I forgot her name again."

"Annette," I helped.

Alex went on with his explanations. "She lives here, too. My cousin Alexander called her and told her that he's coming to visit and gave her my phone number." He went back to his newfound close relative once or twice removed (who was counting?) and excused himself.

She asked him another question, to which he responded, "Yes, I'm married. No, I am--seriousely."

"What's going on here? Do you want me to explain to her that you *are* married? Of course she cannot believe it. So young, only fifty, and already married." I was losing my patience with him, especially in that he really sounded drunk.

"I *am* married. I have a very charming little wifey. Can't you hear her yelling?"

She said something else.

"No, I don't drink. Usually never. But today is a very special day for our country—Halloween," he announced as if he had just invented it.

I couldn't decide what I wanted more—to laugh or cry. I was so glad I never saw him drink; it was not becoming.

He continued, "All these kids keep coming to the door, and you have to drink with all of them. And the mothers! Agnes, you should see those boobs. It's almost like Silicon Valley here today."

"Annette," I corrected. I hated him.

"Who?"

I didn't answer.

Now she was very interested in something.

"No," Alex replied, I was joking about Silicon Valley. Of course we live in Los Angeles, don't worry. Of course you can come to visit when our common cousin Alexander is here. Let me check with my wife when it would be a good evening for you to come. Of course I always discuss everything with my wife." He started sweating.

"Vika, what is our schedule? Do we have a free evening?"

"She can come only on the first Monday. We will be busy the weekend he arrives, and then we are going to Las Vegas on Tuesday. So she has Monday."

Alex got back to Annette.

"My wife says you can come on Monday. I'll give you directions. Ready? You have to take freeway one-oh-one. If you're heading north, let's say coming from downtown, you exit at Big Oak Canyon and turn left. If you are heading south, exit at Big Oak Canyon and turn right. Where are you coming from? Omaha? Who is Omaha?"

"I hope it's a street name!" My heart skipped a bit.

"Omaha, Nebraska? But Nebraska is a state!" It was a second declaration by Alex after declaring Halloween. "Seriously, where are you going to be coming from? LAX?"[4]

"Over my dead body!" Try to guess who screamed that. You guessed right.

Alex was sobering up by the second. "Agnes, how can you be coming from Omaha, Nebraska, for an evening?"

"Don't give her any wrong ideas, or she'll think you're insisting that she come for longer. Just tell her right now that she is not going anywhere! Now I can see why she and her mother were twice removed from your family. They couldn't remove them the first time. Tell her that your wife is a bitch and doesn't like when your close relatives sleep with us because it's incest. Alex, it's not funny anymore. It really looks like your cousin Alexander decided everything for us from Russia. Why doesn't she just buy him an airline ticket and invite him to Omaha, Nebraska?"

My poor Alex was desperately trying to think of something to say to her.

"Vika, what was her name?"

"Annette."

---

4   Los Angeles International Airport

"Listen, Annette, we have a very tight schedule. We will be showing him around on the weekend he comes, and then we're going to Las Vegas on Tuesday. So you can come for Monday only. Also, who is going to take you to and from the airport?"

Annette was not giving up.

"Vika, she's saying that she has never been to Las Vegas, either."

My life was spiraling out of my control, and I hate when that happens. I like to be in control of my life—never of other people's lives, but always of mine.

I grabbed the second phone and firmly said, "Annette, when Alexander is here, he will call you, and we will settle everything then." Then I hung up, and hung up Alex's phone as well.

We sat there and looked at each other, and then we started laughing hysterically. Alex took one glass and gave me another, and we raised them and drank. I knew I had a new story to add to my repertoire. But who would believe all of this? They would say I made it all up. Go ahead and try to make up something like that!

Finally, the big day came. That Saturday morning, Alex drove to the airport and brought Alexander home. I saw them pulling into the driveway and ran outside to greet him. They entered the garage and got out of the car.

I hurried toward him, wanting to give him a welcome hug, but he said, "How come you have two chandeliers in the garage?"

I looked up and regarded the two chandeliers. I had stopped noticing them a long time ago. One we had taken from our condo when the buyers requested that we buy them a better one; the other was one Alex had gotten from a client who asked him to discard it. Alex wanted to trash both, but I always have a hard time throwing things out. I begged him to keep it for those happy times in the future when Danny would buy his own place. Julia would never settle for such "no brand" junk. So that is how it happened that we had two chandeliers in the garage, which made a very strong impression on our guest, very strong indeed. He commented on it every time he found himself in the garage.

We took his luggage and entered our less-than-modest love nest. I had prepared a nice lunch and invited him to eat with us. But he expressly wished to tour the house first. In total silence, he inspected every corner of our four-bedroom, two-bathroom, three-closet, one-pantry, half-attic, no-crawl-space house.

When he finished his inspection and came back to the living room, he said, "If I knew that even Alex could live like this, I would have moved to America, too. You should have invited me a long time ago so I wouldn't have lost all those years." He was so stricken with envy that he couldn't even conceal it.

"You haven't seen anything yet. You cannot fully appreciate America until you see something of it."

"I saw everything I needed to already."

I tried to comfort him as much as I could. "It's not only about what's on the surface. Don't despair, because we have our problems, too. Alex is just an electrician. We don't drive fancy cars, our house is one of the most modest among our group of friends, my jewelry is all fake, and our paintings are all reproductions."

The last two statements weren't true; they were little white lies to support a human being in grief. But he remained inconsolable.

We went to the kitchen to eat. And then came the second bombshell. Alexander was a very big (literally and figuratively) meat eater. My Alex was nearly vegetarian, occasionally eating fish and rarely some chicken. I had prepared salmon with wasabi mayonnaise, mushrooms, and vegetables—my specialty.

I had even bought Alaskan wild salmon for the occasion. I very seldom buy it for us; usually, farm raised will do. But for guests, I buy the expensive one. It's the Russian way. A guest in the house is sacred; the best of everything goes to the guest. Guests sleep in your bed, and you sleep on the floor. That's how it was in Russia. I know it's wrong, and I'm trying to break my old habits. America is a much more pragmatic, and therefore, fair, country. Theoretically speaking, if you don't have a bed for visitors, they have to stay at a hotel. There is no taking advantage of other people.

In any case, I got carried away. It happens every time I compare the two countries.

And that was crisis number two. Alexander came to America to finally eat "real meat," as he referred to beef or pork, because he could not afford it at home. We had not bought beef in years, and when I asked my Alex whether he felt like meat, I meant chicken. So chicken was the meatiest meat we ever consumed.

I saw that our guest was extremely disappointed in his first encounter with us. I ran to the fridge and quickly defrosted some chicken breast strips I kept for salads (lean chicken breast, zero grams of trans fat, zero grams of saturated fat, twenty milligrams of sodium, and only fifty calories for eight strips). Alexander was rather indignant when I offered them to him; he explained to me what *he* calls "real meat." I didn't know what to do. According to my code of conduct, which I inherited from my beloved bubbe, a guest has to be treated as royalty. I wonder if British royalty eat beef for breakfast. I will have to look it up later. They probably do; the Brits are big on steaks. Oh well…

For the first fifty-nine minutes of having our guest in the house, my Alex was mute. He was forming an opinion. His heart was open to love and please, but he did not have a grandmother from whom to learn my code of conduct. He got very upset with me for a) trying to support our guest in his discontentment that my Alex lived better than he had hoped he would and b) trying to find an excuse for why we didn't cook meat for him.

Alex got up and yelled, "We don't eat meat. We eat a lot of other good food. So you will have to suffer with us and make up for it when you are home and can eat your own food."

My heart stopped. His behavior was so rude.

Alexander went to the guest bedroom to unpack, and I called Alex into our bedroom for a talk.

"You know I was absolutely against the idea of giving up three weeks of my life, plus the money to pay for a good vacation. But now he's here, and he is *my* guest. You either treat him as a welcomed guest is supposed to be treated or else. You break my heart, and I will get sick if you continue in this manner. He will eat what *he* likes to eat, not what *you* want him to eat. Is that clear?"

When we met again in thirty minutes for dessert, our guest looked very normal and relaxed. I think Alex's outburst may have even put him in a mood for getting along with us. Go figure. My old friend Maggie (remember M&M?) called it *shockotherapy*.

On the first evening we had Alexander, I told him to call Annette and tell her that we could not take her to Las Vegas, but she could come to visit him here for the evening on Monday. I took this chance because I was sure she would never buy a plane ticket for one evening if we told her she could not stay for at least a week in LA and spend a few days in Las Vegas.

I told him that there was no way she would pay $500 or more for a last-minute ticket to fly here to see him for a few hours. He didn't believe me.

"Is five hundred dollars considered big money for those who live in America?" This is the stereotype the whole world has of Americans: We are made of money, and we should pay, pay, pay for them all.

I proved to be right; she said something came up and could no longer make it. He was utterly dismayed, pressing her for the reason as to why she had to cancel. She promised to call him every evening so they would feel as close as if they were sitting next to each other.

We spent the first weekend of Alexander's stay touring Los Angeles. I planned to take him to the Paul Getty and the Norton Simon Museums, but he rebuffed my idea in favor of going to some stores to buy clothes for him and his family. My Alex adamantly opposed spending his weekend shopping. So I made a compromise. I agreed to take Monday off (that is, if Annette did not change her plans and pop up unexpectedly) and accompany him to a few stores.

By Sunday night, I felt I was coming down with something. I had a fever and felt very low. But, on Monday morning, I took him to a few inexpensive stores I knew, as promised. He agonized over every dollar, and I quickly deduced that he expected me to help him a little. But we had spent so much money already for the airline ticket, hotels, and going out that I decided it was a matter of principle to let him know I was not willing to pay more, even though we *are* Americans. He relinquished and bought a few things.

"Vika, everything I saw today is not as good as I expected and not as cheap as I've been told it would be."

"Alexander, I can take you to nicer stores that carry finer things, but everything will be even more expensive."

"Annette suggested that you take me downtown, not to some cheap made-in-China hole-in-the-wall places, but to the better stores."

"Alexander, dear, I don't want to spend my vacation day driving to downtown LA. Plus, I don't know where those stores are, so you would waste your time with me. We will browse the stores in Vegas."

I started to realize that he would prefer for us to buy him a lot of *schmattes*[5] instead of taking him to Las Vegas and everywhere else. But everything was decided already, and Alex did not want to change our plans. Alexander complained bitterly that he could've bought similar items in Russia for almost the same price, so why did he bother coming to visit us?

Before he came, I went through our closets to find whether we had anything nice we could spare. And so did Greg and Nelly. By the time Alexander arrived, I had amassed several big bags of clothes. After we returned from the shopping spree, I showed him what I had.

"I want you to know that I am poor but proud. I will not take any junk," he declared before even opening a bag.

After giving me this warning, he began an evaluation of the bag's contents. He looked at the Hugo Boss sweater Greg had parted with (have you noticed how clothes have a tendency to shrink after turning forty?) and deemed it out of style by two or three years.

"We are definitely closer to Europe," he said. "And you are definitely behind. By the way," he continued, "as any advanced country, we are having a sexual revolution now."

"What does that mean?"

"Open marriages. I have the two mistresses, and my wife doesn't mind. We even attended a swing party once, but we hated it there and left. They wanted my wife to participate, too. It was so disgusting."

"How very advanced, indeed."

He continued, "I asked Alex whether you are up to this here as well. He said no. We are definitely closer to Europe. He said he doesn't need anybody but you. He said he thinks that you're a jealous woman, so he would not even think of it even if he wanted to, but he does not. He likes everything about

---

5   garments

you. All he wants is to live with you for the rest of his life. That's what he said. He said that even when you—"

"Please stop!" I interrupted him. He made me sick for discussing with me what Alex had told him in a private conversation, man to man. Had he no ethics?

"Does your wife have a lover, too?" I changed the subject.

"No, she said she's satisfied with me."

"Well, I think she's not advanced enough and has to try harder, or you have to force her. Having such an open-minded husband, she must take a lover herself. Progressive is progressive. For God's sake, are you so close to Europe for nothing?"

He kept quiet for a few minutes, trying to comprehend what I had just said. Then he got back to the *schmatte* business.

There were plenty more nice pieces from Greg, but they were too small for Alexander. After rummaging through all the bags, he managed to find a few acceptable items for himself, for his children, and for his wife. I returned the rest to Greg and Nelly when they stopped by that night, and I packed up our clothes that he had turned down to donate to the Salvation Army.

I remembered that Alex had a brand-new, tags-attached, shiny-silver Emporio Armani down jacket. His sister had given it to him as a present a year or two earlier, but it was too big and too shiny for him.

I attempted to give it to Danny when he went skiing, but he took one look at it, then looked at us and said, "I thought you knew me better by now." He fingered the Emporio Armani logo on the front of the jacket. "That is not my name."

As this expensive treasure was taking up one-third of my closet, I offered it to Alexander. He took a deep breath, pulled his stomach in, and closed the zipper. He looked like a very big and very shiny silver balloon. Actually, he looked like a very big, very shiny, and *very* ecstatic silver balloon. He was beside himself with joy. He cried that this one jacket had made up for all his other grievances and made his trip worthwhile.

"What do you mean?" I asked, bewildered. "Didn't we pay for everything not to burden you?"

"Do you think it didn't cost me money? I had to bribe somebody to obtain a visa. I had to bribe my manager to let me take two weeks of vacation this month; I was scheduled for January of next year a long time ago. And I had to bribe my physician, who post-dated a doctor's note that I will be sick two weeks from now so that I could add another week."

Don't I miss my motherland!

When Greg and Nelly left, I collapsed in bed with a nasty flu and told Alex that they would have to go to Las Vegas without me. He was so upset he almost cried.

"I cannot stand him. I will get physical if you're not there. Please, dearest, all you have to do is to stay in bed and rest. Just be there for me."

If my Alex despairs, my heart bleeds. So I called the hotel, canceled the first night (money lost), and added another night. Tuesday came and we were still no closer to departing for Las Vegas. Meanwhile, I was wasting valuable vacation days lying in bed. Alex went to work, and I told Alexander that he had to explore our neighborhood by himself. I drew him a map of how to get to the shopping center and the big plaza and labeled what building represented what store. His English was nonexistent. Not a word. So I pulled two pages from my notebook and wrote two phrases for him to show to somebody if necessary: "Where is the restroom, please?" and "I am lost. Here is the address and phone number."

He folded both sheets and put them in his pocket. I only hoped he would remember which was which. He also asked to borrow our calculator and then left on his mission. I fell into a deep sleep; I was so exhausted by all this nonsense.

He disappeared for six hours, and I was beside myself with worry, to the point where I was about to call the police. I wanted to cry.

I called Alex, and he comforted me. "Vika, are you sure you bought the best travel insurance for him? Then don't worry. He is my relative, not yours. Let me worry. Go back to bed and concentrate on your runny nose."

Our guest finally returned, looking overly excited and rather pleased with himself. He was full of stories. On the way there, he stopped at the closest shopping center and went into our huge supermarket. He spent a full two hours there inspecting every available product. With calculator in hand, he converted the prices from dollars to rubles for every single item they had and compared them to the prices in Russia. That was how he spent the first hour. Then he got to the most important stuff; he entered the shrine—the meat department. He stayed there for an hour calculating figures using the backside of the two sheets of paper with my phrases for his numbers, formulas, spreadsheets, and research. The poor guy who worked there became very nervous and called the store manager for help. The manager asked Alexander something, but we will never know what. Then they called the janitor, who happened to speak Spanish, and he asked Alexander something as well; we will never know what exactly, either. Then they all called for security. At that moment, Alexander showed them my first phrase, and all four of them walked him to the bathroom.

On the way back, Alexander started to work on the deli department but was not too impressed by it because they only had some kind of bologna, which was not what Alexander considered meat, as you might know by now.

The store also had a very nice cafeteria. Alex and I often walked there on Sunday mornings to have a danish and a cup of coffee. Because the food was not kept behind a counter as in all the other departments, Alexander surmised that everything there was complimentary. He took a few pastries and the biggest cup of coffee and helped himself. The employee mopping the floors smiled at him and said something to Alexander as he passed the cashier. I can only imagine what those poor people were thinking when some lunatic came into their store not speaking any recognizable language, writing down some cryptic stuff, and not paying for his food. I explained to him that the coffee and the pastries as well as the soup and salad were self-serve and did not require the aid of a salesperson, but when he got what he needed, he had to pay for it at the cashier. He maintained that he was not as stupid as I thought and that the guy smiled at him the whole time and even walked him out of the store (probably making sure he was really gone). He allegedly knew what would happen if he really had to pay and did not; the security guard would throw him on the floor, handcuff him, and call the police. This is probably what they do in Russia. I dropped the subject; there was no point to it. We had patronized this store for so long that they would have to bite the bullet.

So I asked him what he did after that. He said he walked farther down the road to our big plaza. There was a movie theater, a number of nice restaurants, and a Barnes & Noble, all of which were of absolutely no interest to him. (The bookstore was lucky he didn't know that they had a nice café.) He commented on people's attire and how they were not dressed as nicely as those in Russia. He was surprised. I noted that it was only lunchtime and that people dress casually for work. But he criticized Americans for having all the money in the world and not buying the hot stuff all Russians dream of having but very few can afford. The only thing left that could possibly interest him were a number of vendors with small kiosks. He took them very seriously, picking up each item and thoroughly inspecting it. He reported finding a purse for his daughter that was in fashion that season, but it was not as cheap as he was told it should be in America. I wondered who published the list of American prices in Russia.

On the way home, he decided to stop by our supermarket again; he felt at home there already. When he entered the store, there were more people than in the morning, but the staff recognized him at once. The janitor smiled at him again, followed him to the bathroom, waited for him outside, and walked him to the exit, not letting him approach any department. This spoiled Alexander's impression of that store, but I will not tell them.

All in all, he returned home impressed by the willingness of the Americans he had met that day to try to understand and help him using only body language.

The next morning we were off to Las Vegas. After checking into the hotel, I went directly to bed. Alexander the Great—oops, I meant Alexander the Guest—was ready to conquer Las Vegas. Alex took Alexander to show him some of the hotels on the Strip. I advised that their first stop should be some buffet. They went to the Paris hotel and spent an hour standing in line and two hours eating. Actually, Alexander suggested to Alex that if he was done eating, he could leave and do some gambling and meet him at the buffet exit in another hour. I think he had a meat feast like he never had before. I only hope the buffet did not run out of meat before he was done gorging himself. When they came back a few hours later, he could barely breathe.

We had a free show ticket included in our rate, so Alex took Alexander against his will to see the topless show, seated him in the theater, and told him he would meet him when the show was over. Then he came back to me and crashed. He complained that I was not adamant enough about protesting against his cousin coming to visit.

Neither the show nor the exotic hotels impressed Alexander too much, but the buffet at Paris sure did. The next day, I suggested that they go to the Caesar's Palace buffet and continue exploring Sin City. Is gorging a sin? I think so. We are all guilty of it once in a while. "Forgive me Father for I have sinned…"

I stayed in the room because I was still sick as a dog. I ordered oatmeal and coffee to the room. If our guest saw this disgrace and the bill, he would lose his last respect for me.

Upon their return, Alexander the Guest announced that even though Caesar's Palace is still considered the most grandiose hotel in Las Vegas, it is nothing compared to Paris. Apparently, they didn't even have what he could call real meat. He asked whether I felt any better and if we could go to Paris again in the evening. Considering it was 6:00 p.m. already and they had just finished a three-hour lunch, Alex told him all we would be having for the rest of the night were desserts and tea. We usually don't eat that late, but hospitality is hospitality.

In the morning, my Alex generously offered to go Paris to have breakfast, but when we got there, he broke our guest's heart by going directly to his favorite French bakery.

"Eating a lot is unhealthy in general," Alex chided. "And eating red meat for breakfast is particularly unhealthy. Vika is even paying money not to eat." (He was referring to Weight Watchers.)

Alexander could not believe his ears. When he and I happened to be alone, he asked if it could possibly be true that people pay money not to eat. I said yes. And when he learned how much money it cost me, he was speechless. Just to think how much meat I could buy…So we went to the bakery, and poor Alexander had no choice but to not enjoy three danishes with butter and jam and three cups of coffee with cream.

The next day was Thanksgiving, and we planned to stop by Greg's place on the way home to spend time with the family.

Before leaving Las Vegas, however, we made a long stop at another buffet somebody had recommended to us. It was much cheaper than Paris's and had a huge variety of meat and desserts. Alexander was interested in both, Alex only in the latter. I am not exaggerating when I say we spent three whole hours there. Our guest was preparing himself to survive a five-hour drive with no meat.

We finally made it to Greg's, but oh the horror! It never dawned on me that turkey is not meat in Alexander's world. Nelly cooks a delectable turkey, as you well know, and it was a really beautiful dish this time. But it was not meat! Oh well, he had to deal with some delis and dessert. The worst part was we had to prepare to leave after only forty minutes because I was so unwell, which greatly annoyed our guest.

Just when we were about to leave, Nelly said, "Wait for a few more minutes. Sofia and her bunch are coming. She was thrilled to hear that you would be here. I didn't realize that you two were such dear friends."

Ignoring her snide remark, I replied, "I will stay until they come. How are they doing?"

"They are doing *very* well. That schmuck Neiman has a great job. All of a sudden he is such a big scientist that they even hired a translator to help him work. He flies around the world attending all these symposiums, and Sofia goes with him. And his company pays for her travel expenses, too! Some people know how to survive in style." She looked at my beloved Greg accusingly.

"What about the kids?"

"She is so lucky to have children like them. They are both so well positioned in life. Her daughter is getting married into a very wealthy family, *very* wealthy indeed. What was the point in going to college? But, on the other hand, that's where she met her future husband. And she's not even half as pretty as my Michelle. I told my stupid daughter that going to a good college increases your chances to meet a quality husband, but who listens? Her son became a lawyer. But of course! What else would a nice Jewish boy become to please his mama, except for maybe a doctor? He works for some big movie studio or production company. You should see the car he's driving! My children, who grew up in America, don't drive such cars! And all their friends are such achievers. I really want our children to meet and spend more time together, even if just for the sake of the memory of our parents."

The doorbell chimed, and Nelly ran to answer the door. I heard her shout, "My babies are here! Come, come give me a kiss. You are so big—as big as I am!" (which is very big, if you ask me).

The noise and commotion from their arrival was so unbearable that I realized just how sick I was, yet I gathered my strength and went to say hi to Sofia. She hugged me in spite of all my protests that I was contagious.

I took advantage of the screaming and whispered to her, "I am so glad you are here again."

"So am I. My parents' grandchildren cannot be strangers to each other. I will not let that happen."

"Very well, let's forget it."

"One thing still comes to mind, though. Now that we are more or less established the way Nelly was at the time, I cannot believe that I would consider sacrificing anything for a lousy ten thousand dollars."

"Sofia, what about ten million? Would you break your word to your mother for ten million dollars that doesn't belong to you?"

She laughed. "I would have to think about it. All right, all right, you made your point. Of course it's not a matter of the amount. Nevertheless, I will have to forgive and forget. I must and I will."

"I cannot tell you how happy I am to hear that. Now I can call it a day and go home to enjoy my flu."

I did not wish to discuss this subject with Alex having Alexander the Guest in the car on the drive home, but with just a few remarks and a few knowing glances, we were on the same page. It was unbelievable what an understanding Alex and I had.

I jokingly said, "Alex, what did I do to deserve you?"

He sighed. "I know, poor Vika…" He was grinning.

We were so busy entertaining our guest that we had lost track of things in our everyday life. Alex called Julia a few times from Las Vegas, mainly to compel her to meet with us when we were back. His cousin had not yet seen Julia, so he still hadn't seen anything of importance. But Julia was not to be found. Alex remembered her telling him that she might go out of town for the holiday weekend, but I could tell he was getting nervous.

Thankfully, there was a message waiting from one of her friends when we came home that night. Julia had asked her to call and let us know that she was fine, but one of her friends had gotten in an accident and was being taken to a hospital in another area. Our first reaction was that she herself had gotten in an accident and was in the hospital and didn't want us to worry, so she made up this crazy story. Alex kept trying her cell phone, leaving distraught message after message. We went to bed and held each other, lying there with our eyes wide open. We were paralyzed with fright as the horror was crept into our souls. We knew the peaceful days were over.

I remember quietly praying, "If only she is alive, I don't care about anything else. Oh God, please let her be alive. He will not survive it. And I will not survive his not surviving." And then I said to myself, "But things like that don't happen in real life, only in the movies."

Julia called at 3:00 a.m.

She sounded very merry and told us another nonsensical story about some girl who she was forced to go visit in Sacramento after having a miscarriage. Her speech was strange and inarticulate, but we were so relieved that she was all right that we couldn't help feeling ecstatic. Alex even started crying with relief. Then we went back to bed and lay there in the quiet, thinking and analyzing.

Half an hour later, I said, "She's on drugs again."

"Yes."

❧

PART 4

I DON'T LOVE MY LIFE ANYMORE

CHAPTER 23
COUSIN IS LEAVING, HORROR IS STAYING

Although we tried very hard not to involve Alexander in any of our issues, he could obviously smell trouble when our phone rang at 3:00 in the morning. Alex told him that we were worried that Julia had gotten into a car accident, but it all turned out to be a false alarm.

I was on the phone for hours the next morning trying to figure out the extent of the problem we were about to face. Julia was back in town but did not sound like her usual self. She mentioned having a very bad cold and making an appointment to go see a doctor. I immediately called her doctor and beseeched him to tell me what was wrong with her. He was not permitted to discuss Julia's condition without her consent, so I had to call her back to ask that she allow me to be present during the examination. Fortunately, she agreed. Then I called Alex and told him my plan; I also told him to take a few hours off and come home early to take Alexander to the airport since I would be at the doctor with Julia that afternoon.

Although he should have been preoccupied with packing, Alexander made every attempt to overhear my phone calls and kept probing me to find out what was going on. He was so hopeful that things were not that good with us after all.

I informed him that Julia had a very bad cold, and we were afraid that it had become pneumonia.

He was not easily convinced. "She had a car accident last night, and now she has pneumonia? So which is it?"

"Both," I snapped.

"Regardless," he said, changing the subject, "my luggage is four pounds under the limit, so I can take more stuff."

I had given him my scale, and he weighed himself with and without his luggage to determine whether each of his suitcases held extra weight.

"They won't fine you if your baggage is underweight, only if it's over."

"Well, perhaps I could take some more of the clothes you had."

I was too distraught with Julia to consider anything else. "No, Alexander, those clothes are going to charity. You have plenty already."

He refused to take no for an answer, insisting that he could take more. When Alex showed up looking ten years older than he had only three days before, Alexander tried his case with him. But poor Alexander had to leave America four pounds under-packed. When somebody is on drugs, it affects everybody around that person, even the guest from Russia. I am trying to inject some humor here, but unfortunately, it's not funny at all. The truth is it affects everybody, even your neighbor's gardener's nephew.

The minute they left for the airport, Alex's sister, Kathy, called.

"Where are my Alexes?"

"Your brother Alex went to the airport to kiss the airplane with your cousin Alex."

"Oh, our cousin left, then? I owe you a big favor for having him."

"You bet you do!"

"Vika, Alex called and left a message. Is there anything wrong? Is it Julia again?"

"Yes," I said.

She waited for me to provide her with more details, but I didn't have them yet. "Vika," she finally replied, "you will have this trouble with her all your life. I told him to live his life and at least appreciate finally having a wife like you."

"Kathy, thank you for your kind words, but when drugs are concerned, there are no normal rules of life that can be applied. There is no answer to any of this. Would you give up on your children?"

"I hate this kind of rhetorical question. I would never give up on my children, but there is absolutely nothing you can do. You cannot live their lives for them. And one should not give up on one's life, either. But, no, I will never give up on my children."

"Then there is no answer to it, is there?"

"I guess not."

"Oh well, I really appreciate your trying, dear. I hope you will never have to face these kinds of decisions."

"Vika, if there is anything at all I can do to help—"

"I know, dear. I will let you know," I assured her and hung up.

Even Kathy did not know what to say, and she is one of those few people who usually knows what to do in every situation.

I loved Kathy. First of all, she lived far away, which made her a perfect sister-in-law. Second of all, both times we visited her in New York, she escorted us around Manhattan, taking us to the Metropolitan Opera (my dream come true) and giving us a very insightful tour of Central Park. Third of all, we spoke the same language, she and I, and not only because it was Russian.

I called Julia, but she didn't answer. I then called the doctor's office, and they notified me that she had canceled her appointment. So I did not go to see her doctor after all.

Alex came home from the airport and recounted the last tales of our departing guest, but they were no longer funny. All of a sudden, nothing else mattered—again.

He called Julia, and surprisingly, she answered. He asked me to talk to her; sometimes I could do better than he could. She confided in me that she lost it for a few days, which meant that she had been doing drugs for a few days, but she quickly came to her senses and was sobering up now. She believed that she, unlike real druggies, could always stop. She also revealed that her arm was badly inflamed with an infection and that her car was in the repair shop. She asked me if I could take her to see a doctor in the morning. I said I would.

The next morning, I called my office and begged my boss to give me the day off on such short notice. I drove all the way to her place (it took me a good hour) took her to the hospital, just to wait outside in the parking lot; she refused to let me see her doctor. She returned a while later with her arm dressed in a bandage.

She got back in the car, and I started to drive.

"Your dad asked me to bring you back to our place to spend the evening with us, and then we'll take you home tomorrow. He said you promised to come over."

"I never made any such promise," she asserted. "Besides, I have other things to do."

"Julia, please just tell me what's going on."

With that, she opened the car door and nonchalantly stepped out of the car when I stopped at a red light. Again, till then I thought this could only be staged in a movie.

We did not hear from her for the next month, except for one message she left assuring us that she was all right.

In the meantime, my very old and very good friends came to visit from the East Coast. They were on their way to San Francisco and stopped for the weekend to spend a couple of days with us. Back in Russia, they were my best friends, and their son was Danny's best friend as well. I had not seen them since we all left Russia, and I was delighted to see them, in addition to introducing Alex to them. They got on well together instantly, and we showed them as much of Los Angeles as possible in our short time together.

In the evening, after driving around the city all day, we had dinner in the backyard. Alex put some music on, and our guests jumped up and started swing dancing. They had been taking dance classes for years, and the moves they were doing were amazing. Then my girlfriend dragged Alex onto the makeshift dance floor with them, and he intuitively began stepping to the music—that's how good a dancer he was. It was so refreshing to hear him laugh again. The evening was as delicious as it had always been when Danny, their family, and I sat in their tiny kitchen talking and laughing twenty-some years ago in Russia.

Alex finally reached Julia the next morning. She answered her cell phone and disclosed that she was very sick and probably had pneumonia. Of course, we did not believe one word of what she said—again.

Alex had to go to work; he could not cancel at the last second. He told Julia that we would come get her and then implored me to go see what was going on. I hated the situation he put me in, as he was robbing me of such precious time with my friends. I showed them around some more, and then we drove to Julia's apartment building. She had been living with her boyfriend in a very nice downtown apartment for a few months. I asked my friends to wait for me in the car while

I went upstairs. The door was unlocked, so I headed inside. The place looked uninhabited; I did not understand where all their furniture and belongings had gone. All the blinds were closed, and I couldn't see a thing except for somebody in the middle of the living room. As I came closer and bent down, I saw that it was Julia lying under a thick blanket. She was half asleep and breathing convulsively. Can anything have such power over a human being? Can anything have the ability to transform one into somebody else? They say that having children, being ill, losing a loved one, and war can. But just a pill or powder—can they have such enormous power to transform a beautiful, sweet person into an animal? Only God is supposed to have such power over a human's mind and fate.

She couldn't talk, she didn't recognize me, and she didn't know whether it was day or night. She was dying there. I shook her to attention and asked where her boyfriend was. She whispered that he had just left because he did not want to meet me. I was at a loss for what to do. I could not leave her there alone, and I could not take her with me because I had my friends from my previous life sitting in the car, and it would be painfully embarrassing to let them see her in such a condition. I called Alex, and he started to cry; I did not debate anymore. I lifted Julia, and right at that moment, the door of their fancy apartment flew open and the landlord barged in. He started to scream at me that he would not let us go until we paid any part of what we owed him. At some point he even raised his hand, and I was sure he would hit me. It was a moment I will never forget. How could I let someone drag me through so much mud? How could my life bring me there to that empty apartment with someone's overdosing daughter and her nasty landlord?

I half carried her to the elevator as he trailed us down the hallway. I cannot even blame him; he was probably sick and tired of dealing with these kinds of renters. He had bills to pay, too; they were robbing him, too. Not paying your rent is stealing. From the beginning of time there have been heart-breaking stories about wicked stepmothers, evil landlords, and poor defenseless orphans. Can we please revisit this scenario? She robbed him of his money; she robbed me of my life.

I guided her to the car, asked my friend to move to the backseat where her husband sat, deposited Julia in the seat next to me, and said, "No questions, please." We drove in complete silence. I was burning with humiliation. So much for the new life, new husband, and new beginning. They had seen me in much better conditions being cheerful and fun, when I was unhappily married, yet living a meaningful life.

I got her home and put her in our bed, which was more convenient because she would have her own bathroom in the master bedroom. Also, I had no idea whether she was contagious. She was suffocating with a cough, and I thought she might have pneumonia or something worse. So, just in case, I isolated her. Our visitors occupied the guest bedroom, leaving us to sleep on the sofa in the living room.

The next morning, my friends rented a car and left for San Francisco. We were supposed to spend Sunday together as well, but now I could not wait for them to leave. Would I ever call them again? Would I ever forgive them for seeing me so humiliated?

I cooked chicken noodle soup, made fresh-squeezed orange juice, and scheduled an appointment with Julia's doctor for first thing on Monday. Alex and I collected all our medicine and alcohol and hid them in the garage—again.

In the middle of the night, Julia woke us up because she couldn't breathe and felt like she was burning with fever. We dressed her and took her to the emergency room. We spent a good five hours there; the gatekeeping nurse who decides who goes in first ignored us. Julia started to quarrel with her, threatening to leave. I pulled the nurse aside and asked her to test Julia for drugs when they took her back, which was a big mistake because she never called us. We finally gave up after several hours of waiting and had to go home.

Julia slept through the entire next day. She appeared to be looking better, though. I went to work, and when I entered my cubicle, I kissed the walls. You probably think I mean this figuratively, but I'm completely serious. My little friend, Stella, came to greet me, and I was so overjoyed to see a normal person that I kissed her, and then I kissed the walls. They symbolized a normal life. I used to say that I was very happy because happiness is when you look forward to going to work and look forward to returning home. Now I was half happy—still, not that bad. Actually, I do think it was that bad.

Late that night, Alex woke me up. He said Julia couldn't breathe, and he didn't know what to do. I had taken a sleeping pill that had recently been prescribed to me, and I felt so dizzy when awakened. I told him to call 911 and get her to the hospital. It was the first time I told Alex to do something of that magnitude alone. I fell back into an uneasy sleep until I was awakened again by some commotion. From our bedroom, I peered into the hallway and saw numerous people—the huge boots of policemen on our shiny hardwoods and medical personnel with a gurney. It felt as if my precious, serene place was being raped.

In a few hours, Alex came back alone. Julia was kept at the hospital for a procedure to suck fluid from her lungs. She had a horrible type of pneumonia, and they started her on antibiotics straightaway. According to Julia, it was not the first time she had ended up in the hospital with lung problems in the last few weeks. We were so penitent for suspecting her of some wrongdoing, while she was legitimately sick all that time.

In the morning, Greg called to check in, but I hadn't the energy to talk to him. I groggily told him that we were still asleep because we had underwent a very hectic night and that we were not going in to work that day. He called a few hours later and was resolute in his desire to know what happened. After learning of Julia's advanced case of pneumonia, Greg offered to find any doctor and pay any amount of money if necessary to help the poor girl get better. He was so heartbroken for us and for Julia. My Greg is a very kind and giving person when Nelly is not around. After he discusses things with her, which he always does, he can often change his perspective. But, to be fair to him, he will not change his opinion when it comes to his principles. We thanked him profusely and professed we would do everything that was needed ourselves, but it was comforting to have a big brother with so much goodness in him.

When we went to visit Julia, she detailed her recovery process, which consisted of remaining there for a few days and then moving to detox when she was a little better. I had no idea what that meant. She explained that it referred to cleansing your system of drugs and toxins over a period of a few weeks.

"What drugs? Didn't you have a cold and then pneumonia?"

"I've been doing drugs for some time, but I'm fine now. As you know, I can always stop anytime I want. I am feeling better already, and don't you start again. I don't want to hear it right now."

Having no clue what to make of it, we went home. The minute we opened the door, the phone rang. Greg was calling to get an update. He was on his way to see us. He was so compassionate, so worried. When he arrived, he said that he had already consulted with some doctor friend who recommended a very good pulmonologist. His friend advised that she probably had pleurisy, if not worse. I had no intention of making a fool of my beloved brother, but there was no way of telling him the truth. He came from the normal world I used to belong to, and his perception of troubles was different. He would not understand even if I tried to explain. And (and it's a big *AND*) there was no way I would ever let Nelly find out. The whole world would know immediately, as it's always imperative for her to be the first to break the news. Plus, since I let everybody know that I had reached the point of my happy ending, I was not ready to unveil the story about my second major failure. So we sat there gawking at the emotional Gregory like two idiots.

The next night, Alex went to visit Julia. I said I did not want to see her. Oh God did I want to add *ever* to the end of that statement.

He came home with a pack of More Reds, which he used to smoke. We ensconced ourselves in the longue chairs in our backyard, and he filled me in on more details as we smoked. Ben, the new boyfriend she had met at AA meetings, was the one who introduced her to heavy drugs. Prior to that, she had never before taken serious drugs—only light ones. (Alex was always so naive when it came to his daughter.) But that evil man put her on heroin or on crack or on cocaine; I cannot remember which, and I still don't know the difference for the life of me.

Initially, she injected it into her veins, but then they got infected, which was why I had to take her to the hospital, where they did some treatment to her arm. She tried again after her arm healed, and again, her veins got inflamed. So the poor darling was left with no other choice than to inhale it. They burned the substance and then inhaled it somehow. I am aware that I sound stupid and illiterate, but I don't want to educate myself about all of this, however closed-minded that might sound. So after she started smoking this stuff, she was repeatedly admitted to the hospital with breathing problems. They extracted fluid from her lungs, put her on heavy antibiotics, and released her. It was a vicious cycle.

Alex was so bitterly upset about Julia becoming a heavy drug addict after not being a heavy drug addict, all of which was not her fault, of course. He said Julia asked me to send her something to read. I gave him my favorite, *Pride and Prejudice*, and he took it to her.

In a couple of weeks, Julia was discharged, and we went to the hospital to pick her up. She stayed with us for a week; I fed her chicken soup, pomegranate juice, and lots of vitamins. I shifted my hours to arrive at work later and stay later, while Alex went to work incredibly early in order to return earlier so that she was under our constant watch. But who knew what she was taking? She took so many pills that there was no way for us to keep track.

She asked me to give her everything I had by Jane Austen. She had gotten hooked on Austen, just as I had years ago. I had all six novels, of course. On Saturday morning, I went to the store and bought the five-hour BBC miniseries, the best version of *Pride and Prejudice* ever. I used to order it from the library, but this was a good excuse to own it. I curled up next to her in bed, and we watched it all Saturday long. We could not stop it and leave some for the next day; we had to finish it, as if we didn't already know how it would end.

I called Alex in and asked him to join us.

"Is it *Pride and Predators* again?" He was a big fan of National Geographic.

"Papa, *Pride and Prejudice*, not *Pride and Predators*. Let's watch it together. You'll love it."

Alex lay down next to us, and for a brief moment, we were one happy family.

Five minutes into the movie, Alex said, "Why are the brides pregnant? Brides could not be pregnant at that time." He was referring to the plump Jane and Elizabeth Bennet.

"They're not pregnant, just a little chubby," I corrected him.

"He could do much better than that…that guy…mister what's his name…Colin Firth."

"Mister Darcy," Julia chimed in.

"I simply cannot take it," he interjected after only ten minutes. "Nothing's happening. Is there any plot whatsoever? And what language do they speak? It's not English! I don't understand a word."

"Alex, it *is* English—as opposed to what we speak, you and I."

"OK, girls, I have to leave you. You will have to tell me how it all ends this time. Last time Vika watched it, she said they all got married—all of them, the entire crew." He got up from the bed and began humming as he exited the room.

We enjoyed the rest of our cozy, comfortable Saturday together. The next day, however, it all ended. In the morning, Julia announced that she felt much better and had to go back home. We knew she would get together with that guy again, and he would provide whatever she started to crave, so we were unwilling to let her go. She was absolutely adamant about leaving; she even called for a taxi. Alex attempted reasoning with her, saying that we would take her home if she insisted, but if she left, he would never see her or speak to her again—ever. She would not listen to a word he was saying. During our long ride, he continued threatening her that she had no father anymore. But she paid no attention to his claims; she only cared about searching for the necklace she had dropped in the backseat. Once she found it, she looked content. I could not believe that only yesterday we had lain in bed together watching *Pride and Prejudice*.

On the way back home, Alex admitted that letting Julia go was a type of catharsis, giving him the closure he needed to move on with his life and ours.

"I cannot survive these ups and downs every day. I don't want to die. I love you and my life with you, and I want to live my own life, too. I am very thankful to you for being so supportive."

The first thing I did when we got home was print a big sign and then stuck it to the fridge: *We have no control over our children's lives. Let's live ours.*

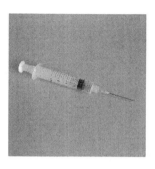

CHAPTER 24
LET'S LIVE OUR LIVES

Before, when Julia was all right, she always made a big deal about Father's Day. She would buy an expensive gift and write very expensive words and promises on a very cute card. Alex kept them all. They all looked so ironic now. I tried to get him back to our normal routine, but the last few weeks had almost killed us.

In the years when Julia was "warm," she forgot about Father's Day and anything else, so on that Father's Day, I gave Alex a gift myself—a membership to my gym. Honestly, I was being selfish. I thought if he started going there religiously, he would make me go there, too. My schedule was averaging only once a month. And even though my membership was three times less than Alex's per month, his averaged out to be cheaper, considering that he was going there three to four times a week. So I started going with him at least twice a week. I'd rather walk around our lake, but companionship is companionship. Alex implemented a bodybuilding routine, although his body was perfect already. Every time I see a French bulldog I think of Alex because he has the same slim, but masculine body—arched, lean, and strong legs. I usually exercised for half an hour, and then I went to the Jacuzzi and steam room. Now, I know why men like the public Jacuzzi—it can turn any man on—but I've always hated it. Have you seen the people at the public Jacuzzis, especially when the middle-aged group is trying to soothe their sore bodies? They know every jet there and its exact location. The elderly, overweight lady next to me was relaxing in her usual spot between three jets after water aerobics. She positioned her lower back against the lower middle jet, then she tried to position her sore right heel against the second nozzle three feet to the right and six inches higher than the middle one, and finally, she located her sore left knee against the third jet two feet to the left. Another gentleman was stretching awkwardly to reach two jets simultaneously, one for his neck and one for his knee. The Kama Sutra paled in comparison. I could easily massage my lower back and heel at once because of my past yoga experience.

After the gym, we went out to have lunch. Those days were our mini vacation. We returned home, read our motto on the refrigerator, and went on with our life.

Danny dreadfully worried me, too. He had graduated from college with honors, got a good job, and was being paid well, and then, all of a sudden, he became a certified scuba diving instructor and went to Thailand for soul-searching. He let his apartment go, sold his new furniture for nothing, and left his big red truck next to our house, which Alex drove for a few minutes once a week on the "garbage out" days to keep it running.

By the time all of this drama happened with Julia, Danny had been working for a year as a scuba instructor on a practically uninhabited island in Thailand. I commanded myself not to think of all the things that could happen to him because I was afraid to attract troubles by even thinking about such possibilities. My grandma's story haunted me. I remember jumping from sleep one night and crying out to a scared Alex that something had just happened to Danny. He comforted me, assuring me that Danny was a self-sufficient and sensible man who would never jeopardize his life. I went back to sleep holding Alex's hand. Danny came home for a short vacation to take care of some business here. Imagine, a vacation to America from Thailand. How trivial is that? While he was here, he told me that he had been injured during one of the expeditions and was admitted to the hospital there. I am absolutely positive his injury happened that night, or rather, that day, because it was daytime in Thailand. I did not tell him anything because he would only laugh at me.

Sometimes I went on for months and months without hearing from him. Every night, before going to bed, I looked out the window at his red truck; the sight of it warmed my heart and made me feel closer to him. Nobody knew what I was going through. In our household, it was all about Julia. It was Julia, Julia, Julia, day and night. Alex was very supportive when I was worried about Danny, but from his point of view, Danny was better off living on the beach in Thailand than Julia who was constantly on the verge of overdose in America.

So we posted this sign and were determined to live our life. When I try to remember those years, I also remember the parties, vacations, projects at work, movies, and theaters. I don't know how we managed to compartmentalize our life. There was life, and there was horror, and they lived together.

CHAPTER 25
FROM LEMONS TO LEMONADE

We did not utter a word about her for many months. I knew Alex had her in mind around the clock, but there was nothing to talk about. Our daily routine resembled that of the "normal" life we used to have before, although I cannot name one solid year of no troubles with her before, either. Sometimes I looked at Alex and could see how he had aged that year. He became absolutely white, and his marbled face was covered with wrinkles, but he still did sixty to eighty pushups every morning and was watching his meals as usual. As for me, I gained some weight again, not too much, but I could not lose it for the life of me. I was so very upset about it. My image had always been that of a baby-faced, slim woman. Alex was so taken with all his problems that he either did not notice how much weight I had gained or didn't care about me anymore. I think luxuries like love or sex or socializing had lost their importance to him. When I complained to him that I hated to look in the mirror, he said, "Don't worry, dearest, fatties are kindies." Whatever happened to his hating meat and fat women? He changed his taste to comfort me. That's my Alex.

Then came yet another blow: Alex lost his job. He was almost the last one to be laid off—that was how much they valued him. Long before it happened, I tried to talk him into starting his own electrical business, because, being over fifty, it would be almost impossible to find a new job if he lost his current position. But he always told me that he'd rather work harder physically than psychologically. Being a very responsible person in everything, he kept telling me that he hated pressure and responsibilities.

Not to concentrate on our misfortunes, I decided to take action. Determined to take this new lemon life threw us and make lemonade, I made an announcement.

"Alex, we are starting a small business—a very small business, just the two of us."

"May I ask what business? Do you have a new hobby again?"

"An electrical business. Isn't that what you know best? Don't you always complain that you have to turn down numerous bigger jobs offered by your own customers because you are working full time? Now you don't. This is the American way! It's actually a blessing in disguise that you finally lost your job."

"You know, you have a talent of twisting facts."

"It's called being an optimist. I will not let you go on unemployment for years and slip into depression. I will not let you have so much free time to worry about Julia. I am starting a business."

"Good luck, Vika. Let me know if you need some help."

His negative reaction did not discourage me. You already know what happens when I set my mind to something. The hardest thing was coming up with a killer name. Alex refused to talk seriously about it, and I had to decide on this all-important issue myself. I combined our names and came up with Alvy Electric. The rest was a piece of cake.

I printed tens of flyers, ordered business cards, sent letters to his existing clients, advising that "I, Alex Lansky, am starting my own business and would appreciate your referring me to any of your friends who need a dependable [as they all know] electrician." Meanwhile, I started going door-to-door in our neighborhood handing out the flyers. I knew what would attract people. In the flyer, I wrote, "I, Alex Lansky, guarantee my work, and every contract will state the number of months or years for which I will come back and fix it for free." He always did it anyway. He really took pride in his work.

People started calling for Alex's services, especially our neighbors. When something happened, they would just come knocking on our door. Once I was tapped out in our own neighborhood, Alex would not allow me to go to strangers' houses on my own, so he joined me in the evenings and on weekends. In three months, I could afford to hire our next-door neighbor's teenage son and his girlfriend to spread flyers.

Long story short, in nine months, Alex had to hire three more electricians to handle the increased workload. He barely broke even after paying their salaries. In the evening, after finishing my work, I helped with the payroll—yet another skill I had to acquire. For a year, he did not bring home a dollar. But he was busy and happy as the business continued to grow, and I was happy, too.

Finally, one Saturday, he came home earlier than usual.

"Vika, dress as if you were going to the Russia area and get in the car—quick. They will be closing."

"Who will be closing?"

"Get anything designer on and let's go. I'll take a shower; it will take five minutes. You have to be sitting in the car by then. I called them, and they are waiting."

"Who's waiting? Can you tell me what's going on?"

"You'll see. I wanted it to be a complete surprise, but I don't have the time and brains for all of that. I should've consulted Sigismund."

Completely bewildered, I found my most stylish outfit and grabbed the Louis Vuitton clutch my friends collectively gave me for my birthday a few years before. I thought someone had invited us to go out.

When we arrived in the Russian area of town and parked at the big shopping center plaza, he went directly to the jewelry store we had widow shopped at for years whenever we happened to be in the neighborhood. When we entered, it was almost like a scene from *Pretty Woman*, or any other Cinderella story. They had several cases filled with diamond rings waiting for me on the counter. Boy was I glad I managed to squeeze in a manicure that week! Otherwise, I would have been quite embarrassed. Additionally, there was a couple we knew in the store, and she was trying earrings, so we really made an entrance.

The next half hour was somewhat painful. I was torn between being money-smart and street-smart. I knew Alex had finished his first big job and was finally getting paid, but the customer was delaying payment for months and we could barely make ends meet to pay our employees. Nevertheless, he had decided to spend his first substantial personal paycheck on the engagement ring he still owed me after all these years. On the one hand, it was very irresponsible, and even stupid, to spend his first paycheck on jewelry. On the other hand, I remembered my grandma, who never owned even costume jewelry, telling me, "Never tell the man that his gift is too much for you. You refuse your husband's gift once, then twice, and then he remembers that you are not too valuable if you don't deserve anything of value."

What really played a major role in my decision was the lady who was there before us surreptitiously moving closer and watching as I examined the rings. So I tried to pretend that buying a diamond ring was actually a routine practice for me. Finally, Alex asked the jeweler whether they could wait another ten minutes for us to decide. They gladly agreed. He hurriedly pushed me outside and said, "Vika, since we are here already, we will spend money today, anyway. Why don't you take it seriously, not concentrate on price, and pick something you will enjoy for years to come. I told them my price range on the phone, so everything on the table is in that range. Just relax and choose something you really like."

With that, we went back inside and bought the ring—the one I've been admiring for years.

When we saw Greg and Nelly the next weekend, she noticed the ring right away. "Even Vika is well-off now," she exclaimed. "In the end, almost every husband I know succeeds. One has to think big." And she looked at Greg.

Alex saw me hurting for Greg. "Actually, Nelly, it was Vika who thought big, as usual. Some wives have vision."

But the reason Alex's business had withstood was due to the fact that he was a workaholic, a very organized person, and very good with customers. The achievement was entirely his. All I did was just nudge him a little.

CHAPTER 26
REHABS, REHABS, AND MORE REHABS

A year after the night when Julia returned to her place, she called us to ask whether we would pay for her to go to rehab. We were so exhausted from dreading the day when that horrible conclusive phone call would finally come that we said yes right away. She went to some place in Palm City, and we sent them the payment for the first month. She called us that night to convey her profound gratitude and determination to get it right this time. She also asked if we were available to visit her over the weekend to attend their support meeting, join them for lunch, and bring her some pocket money to buy goodies when she had a craving. Alex could not wait to see her again. He wanted me to go with him, but I said that I would never go to such a place. I know it is wrong. I know it is closed-minded. But I just couldn't bring myself to do it. I felt too strongly about this ongoing saga to pretend that it was just a regular parents' weekend.

So Saturday came, and he went to visit her. When he came back that evening, he was glowing. He gushed about how gorgeous she looked and how everybody loved her (after the three days she had spent there), telling him what a wonderful daughter he had. Her roommate, who had been there for a few months already, was the daughter of a famous doctor. Julia became fast friends with her and was very happy to find a companion in an unfamiliar place. She swore they would stay friends forever. Alex had lunch with them and then attended the meeting, where he learned that if people do drugs, it is not their fault; they are special who everybody has to be kind to and support. Finally, he found the proof that everything she had done with her life, every bad judgment, was not her fault. I couldn't disagree more. But I chose not to argue and was happy to see him happy, although I had no faith in her after all these years. There are some people who, having ten possible paths, will always pick the worst one; it's called having bad judgment. Maybe this is why they are on drugs…

How could he fall into the same pattern of hope, disaster, and a broken heart again and again?

Three days later, Julia called. Alex was working late, so I had to answer. She was very nice and warm. When she was like that, I felt for her, the poor lost child, kind and silly. She admitted that she was a little upset with her roommate, whose mother had spent days there, taking her out to lunches and on shopping trips. Every day they would bring back bags of expensive clothes and jewelry, and it made Julia feel inadequate. She went on to say that the girl's mother had even promised to buy a Mercedes for her daughter if she stayed in rehab for another three months. She complained, even cried, to me that the other parents pampered all the girls her age, and she felt so deprived.

I had no idea how to respond. On the one hand, I knew that I did not have to upset her and that we had to support her in what she was doing. On the other hand, everything she was saying went against all that I believe in. She was thirty years old. I had a son in middle school when I was thirty; I took good care of him, my finances, and myself. My grandma worked as a maid when she was eight. It was stupid to make such a comparison; I was comparing apples and oranges. Or was I? If Julia was an orange and needed special treatment in life, then why should my bubbe be treated as an apple—a rotten apple? She was just as pretty as Julia, if that counts so much according to her and Alex. But my grandma never complained; she was too busy taking care of everything and everybody.

"Julia, we paid this institution the money we were going to spend for vacation. We cannot do better."

"Do you realize that you have traveled so much already, while I was never out of the country? Do you think *that* is fair?"

"Julia, whatever I have in life, I earned it myself. When I was thirty, I did not even dream of traveling. Russia was a sealed country. But now the whole world is open to you. Work hard, save money, and travel. What's stopping you?"

"Do you know how little money all these programs pay people like me? If I were making your salary, I would travel, too!"

"Julia, have a nice day. I will tell your dad you called."

When Alex came home, he called her back. He talked very kindly and soothingly to her. He explained to her that all she had to worry about was getting back on her feet, and then everything would fall into place. His voice was apologetic and defensive. He promised to visit again over the next weekend and said good-bye.

He looked very upset following their conversation. He was riddled with pain and regret for her. He even likened her to that of an orphan, believing if she had a strong family behind her, she would not be so weak and confused. He told me that Julia's old friend, Jane, had called her, and while they were chatting, Julia complained again about her roommate. Apparently Jane was surprised that Julia had to struggle so much to survive, as she knew for a fact that I was making a six-figure salary, and therefore, Alex could afford to help her a little more. "What are you talking about?" Alex had asked Julia.

"I wish she did, but she doesn't make six figures—not even close."

I was livid that he had the nerve to apologize to her because I didn't make six figures. "Alex, what if I were? Would I have to apologize for that? Why don't they, both of them, work as hard, learn to be tight with money, and then pay for my vacation! Wouldn't that be nice?"

"Vika, why are you so upset? People are different. Some are like us—capable of taking care of themselves, hardworking, and responsible. And others are weaker, confused, and have ADD or something like that."

"Oh, how convenient! As long as you find the term, you can count on everybody around you and blame everything on ADD. Alex, listen to me carefully. Once a person is over eighteen years old, he or she is responsible for his or her own life. You want to live well? Do what it takes to live well. You want to live miserably? Do what it takes to live miserably. If Julia wants to be normal again, she will have to fight whatever she has to fight. I don't even want to know what exactly because it is her fight. If she is not determined to climb out of that ditch, so be it. Neither shopping nor trips will help. Only one person can help Julia—and that is Julia."

"Vika, this is not what her counselors told me. Everybody must give them support."

"I respectfully disagree. For years, we tried different things. She lived with us, we paid for her, and we talked to her for hours. It is only up to her."

"If it were your own daughter…"

Eight days later, a representative from the rehab facility called to advise us that Julia was very upset with them and was on her way out as we spoke. I compelled them to keep her forcefully, but they said they were absolutely not allowed to withhold her against her will. I asked what would happen to our money and whether they would reimburse us for the rest of the month. They would not offer a refund of any kind but would credit her for the fifteen days should she return later. That's what I call a profitable business!

We were so heartbroken! If such places existed, wouldn't you expect them to be able to hold people who are incapable of making proper judgments by themselves? Wouldn't they need to lock them in on the days when withdrawal is killing them? But, no, it was a free-will deal. But what will and what common sense could you expect of a person in such condition? It was a vicious circle.

So Julia left the rehab center and called us from home. She said that she did not get along with the rehab personnel, as her desire to rest interfered with their regimented schedule and strict discipline. According to her, they were mean to her, and her roommate was getting on her nerves. She tried to convince us that she was absolutely cured and determined to start looking for a job. We urged her to go back and use her remaining credit at the facility, to which she said, "I ain't no patient of theirs ever again." So ended her stint at Palm City rehab.

Julia soon found a job as a front-desk clerk at another doctor's office, which she was very excited about. She loved the doctor, who happened to be a very pretty and stylish (most importantly) woman. And she adored Julia—which went without saying. After only a week, Alex related that Julia was doing just great at the office; she worked hard to organize all the files that nobody had attended to in years. She was becoming a very good friend of the doctor and even helped her with patients. When Alex called his sister, Kathy, and effused about Julia's appointment, you would think Julia was becoming a doctor. I knew how sharp Kathy was, so just knowing what she was thinking right then comforted me.

In three months it was over. Julia made a big scene and got herself in trouble. Alex was very upset, as if he expected something different this time. He begged me to call her and talk her into going back and apologizing. I finally relented and called her to find out what had happened. She was rather indignant about the whole situation as she detailed the following series of events: One patient, a pregnant woman, came to see the doctor for minor bleeding. The doctor examined her, gave her some medicine, and sent her home on bed rest. The next day, the patient came back and told Julia that she was feeling worse. The doctor was not in the office, as she had been called to the hospital to deliver another baby. Julia paged the doctor and told her that the patient from the day before had returned and that she looked really bad in her opinion. The doctor asked to speak to her assistant because she was not at liberty to discuss patients with Julia. Feeling inferior, Julia snappily pointed out that if the patient were to have a miscarriage, the doctor would be responsible for it, and she, Julia, would advise the woman to sue the doctor. The doctor promptly fired Julia and then kindly asked her to call the nurse.

When Julia told me all of this, I thought she was hallucinating again. How could it all be possible? Did she really think she had become a doctor? Did she really think the doctor would keep her after that? I inquired as to the outcome of the patient. She said the nurse called 911, and the woman was taken to the hospital, where she was probably fine. Or not. She said that was not the point. Now this was becoming interesting.

"What *is* the point, then?" I asked.

"The point is that the doctor was negligent and had a bad attitude. I warned her the day before that I did not like the way that lady looked and felt, but who listened? Do you think I should sue her if I find that lady? Do I have a case?"

"I would not know, dear. I have never sued anybody in my life. I make money a different way."

"Well, I will have to consult somebody, then. I know a guy who looks for cases like this and gives them to his lawyer friend and gets some kickbacks. Also, Victoria, do you think it's legal that she fired me just like that?"

"I wish I could help you, but I can't. I know nothing about it."

"You *are* no help. I don't understand why papa is always telling me, 'Talk to Vika. Ask Vika.' You are not all that smart and knowledgeable."

That evening, I told Alex that I didn't like how Julia sounded; her voice was hoarse, and she was very aggressive. He said he had talked to her earlier in the morning, and she sounded just fine.

I don't know what the real sequence of events was after our conversation, but according to Alex, Julia called the doctor and apologized. The doctor accepted her apology and allowed her to come back to work; however, the doctor gave Julia her two weeks notice the following week. The doctor reasoned that the office was not doing well financially, and she was forced to lay off Julia because she was the last to join the staff. Julia inquired as to whether she could apply for some kind of unemployment after working there for three months, and I told Alex not to involve me because I didn't know.

I was sick and tired of all this nonsense. If he wanted me to help him, he had to stop pretending that she was normal and admit that she was not just plain unlucky all the time. His complete naïveté insulted my intelligence. If he was not willing to do so, he had to stop talking to me about her all together. That was the deal. And the next few months were quiet and uneventful, as far as I was concerned. But something was cooking, of course.

∽

CHAPTER 27
VISITING THE PAST

Alex could not take any time off because he was afraid to leave Julia without controlling her for a day, and I was losing vacation days, so I decided to do something really drastic. I decided to go to the city where I was born and spent the first half of my life. After the collapse of the Soviet Union, it became a separate country from Russia. I was not sure whether it was a good idea or not to visit there, but it sure was drastic all right. It would be the first time that I took a vacation without Alex. He mentioned a few times that I should not do it, that it was dangerous to go there on my own, but I just knew that if I didn't break the vicious cycle at home, something horrible would happen either to me or to us. Plus, I was leaving him for only one week.

Off I went, and before I knew it, I found myself in my city's airport. And through the customs window, I saw all my old friends who had come to welcome me. And at that second, I knew I had done the right thing!

They took me to see the city; it had become very beautiful in the past fifteen years. I started crying the second I began to recognize the streets. As we passed the intersection where my ex-husband, Danny, and I had lived for the last few years before we left the Soviet Union, I wept. It all just came rushing back, even after all those years! It was as if the past fifteen years had never happened. I could not reason with myself that it was not the same city, not even the same country, and moreover, not the same family who I belonged to now.

When we passed the bus stop by our apartment building, I could picture Danny catching the bus to school. It all was there; it was like a time machine, and I had traveled fifteen, twenty, twenty-five years back.

I stayed with my old friend, Olga, in the city center in the building where I spent my entire childhood and almost all of my adult life at my parents' home before the three of us got our own place. It was extremely convenient. The country was still behind a very solid iron curtain—almost nothing had changed in that respect. I could not break this spell; I *had* traveled back in time.

All my friends were so attentive and kind and so intelligent and noble. I feared how much I would miss them when the time came to leave again. But that would be later, and now I was just breathing the air of my youth. It was intoxicating; it was enchanting.

From what I saw or heard, I realized how sick the system had become there—beautiful city, beautiful people, but an ugly system.

On my second day there, I escaped my friend's kind attention and ran away. I had a date. I went to the intersection where I usually waited for Danny while holding his violin. A few little children, who were the age Danny was twenty years ago, were coming in my direction; one of them could have been my Danny. I crossed the street and went down to the school building. I sat on a bench until the next session ended; the bell rang and the little ones started pouring out of the school. I could actually see my Danny running outside for his break. He saw me, screamed with surprise and joy, ran to me, and joined me on that bench, as we often did together. I had a danish ready, and he grabbed it as usual. I hugged him while he ate and filled me in on the day's events.

Oh, God, I thought, *please don't let this break end. Hello, my little prince, how have you been? I miss you so much. You are telling me what happened today; let me tell you what happened during the last twenty years. You think we are inseparable, don't you? But some mean fairy cursed us, and we almost don't see each other anymore. Oh, don't cry, my darling; I didn't mean to upset you. Don't worry, it will pass. We will be just fine. Just be happy, with or without me around you. Please, God, please, grandma, save my Danny; let him have a meaningful and satisfying life.*

The bell rang again.

All right, my darling, it's time to go back—you to class, I—to twenty years later. We'll be just fine, I promise.

I started back to the city center. Passersby looked curiously at this middle-aged woman who was walking and crying and not trying to conceal it. Were they from twenty years ago or from today? Did it matter? I just walked and walked, and remembered, and walked and remembered some more. It took me weeks after I returned to America to realize why I ventured back there to my old city, to my past: I was searching for myself. I missed Alex badly, but he was on another planet and so was Julia. And my little Danny, my little prince, was here with me on this planet. He was mine again.

When Olga saw my swollen face, she did not ask questions; she understood. She had gotten used to seeing me cry for the first few days of my visit. She rationalized it as being overtired from jet lag. Maybe it was.

One more thing I had to do was visit my babushka Leeza's grave. Olga drove me there but stayed in the car to allow me privacy at her gravesite. It took me some time to find it. When I saw her picture, I started weeping again. We met as grandma and granddaughter who have not seen each other for many years; we hesitated, we remembered each other, and then we just talked. Actually, I did all the talking, and she just listened. While I was pontificating about the throes of my life, I supposed that she was thinking that all my misfortunes were not real misfortunes, that I was spoiled and weak, and that my experiences were nothing compared to what she endured. Maybe she was a little disappointed that I was not as strong as she was, but she did not say anything about it.

When I stopped, I knew exactly what she was thinking: Everything is not that bad. Danny is alive and sound; I am healthy and self-sufficient. (She always emphasized the importance of being self-sufficient.) Greg was also fine, even though I wasn't overly fond of his wife. Family is family, and you must accept your family as it is; you cannot divorce your family.

She mentioned the end of my first marriage, but that was just as well. "You'll survive," she said. It was her favorite phrase. Whenever we scraped our knees or developed a sore throat she usually "comforted" us by saying, "You'll survive."

"Just remember one thing," she added. "Don't compromise your values, or you will pay for it. Don't go against your principles, and everything will become simpler."

"Bubbe, what do you mean? What am I to do?"

"You will know. You'll just know."

I felt so much better. All my problems faded. I kissed the medallion on my grandma's tombstone and promised to be back soon—maybe in ten years. She promised to watch over us and told me to stop dramatizing everything. She reiterated that when a person survives war or hunger or the death of a loved one, then he or she realizes how very few things there are that really matter.

"So, see, Bubelah?" (She always called us *bubelah* when we were little.) "You are just fine. And I am very glad to see that. And Greg is just fine as well. Thank God, it could be much worse. Go and enjoy everything and anything you can still enjoy."

It is not entirely comforting when somebody plays down your problems. But my grandma is not just anybody. And I did feel better.

"I told you that jet lag would pass and you would be all right," Olga said in the evening when she saw me laughing.

Yes, it was some jet lag.

And then my real recuperation started. Olga and I walked all day long. We walked to the theater to see a play and to the farmer's market to eat real wild strawberries with real farmer cheese! We stopped at the cafés to have coffee and snacks, and we walked to visit old friends. I couldn't get enough of it. (We don't walk too much here in America.)

Olga also drove me to the village where Greg and I spent our summers. We knocked on door after door of the old houses trying to find anybody I knew, but all of the older people had died, and all of the younger people didn't live there anymore. Unfortunately, it was all run-down now, so we went to the forest. I knew every meadow and every hill; I knew exactly where to find porcinis, where to find chanterelles, and where to find blueberries. I was ecstatic. We filled our big bag with different types of mushrooms in a couple of hours. We ate all the blueberries we could find until our faces were blue. We took pictures of each other, and we laughed at nothing. Then Olga spread a starched tablecloth on the grass by the lake and put down a very delicious homemade lunch and a bottle of wine, with crystal goblets. She was very poor according to the American definition, but a very dignified person—never one word of complaint. We raised our glasses to good times with old friends and each drank a full glass of wine. We felt like nothing had changed and were transported back to a time when we were young and careless.

Then she said, "Something is missing—some minor things like the husbands we both had at the time and our children running around us. All the rest is just as it was twenty-some years ago when we sat here the last time."

"Let's not spoil it, Olga. Let's just enjoy this time to the fullest. It is very unhealthy and unnecessary to be nostalgic. We were not too happy then. We just miss our youth, that's all." I refused to feel melancholy about anything. This was the part of my trip to my past I wanted to enjoy most.

On the first of September, my graduating class met on the steps of our high school. They had organized a reunion just to meet with me! Some even traveled from other cities. It was so generous of them! We hugged and cried and carried on, all while taking hundreds of pictures. Then we all went to a restaurant and reintroduced ourselves. We had a nice dinner, but the real reunion started when we all went back to Olga's place, which was just around the corner from the school and the restaurant. We continued to drink and laugh and reminisce into the wee hours of the morning, promising to meet again soon. I loved every minute of it. I was so rich. Such quality people surrounded me when I lived in Russia, and now my new life in America was so full. And my Alex was home waiting for me. I was one lucky lady.

I returned home completely reenergized. I told Alex that vacations were invented to help us survive our horrors. They put everything in a different perspective, and this particular trip kept me running for another six months. I had hundreds of pictures and went through them time and again. I had reconnected with my old dear friends, and I started calling and e-mailing them again. It was as if I had gulped some fresh air. And was I glad to be back in America! Everything is right here compared to that old country of mine where everything is wrong, except for some dear, dear people.

PART 5

TRYING TO SAVE
WHAT WE HAD

CHAPTER 28
SOME BREAK AND SOME VACATION!

Alex probably called Kathy and secretly begged her to borrow Julia from us so that he could take a breather. He did not tell me about it; he knew I hated when people put their problems on others.

Kathy had a husband and two children of her own. She had her hands full. They are crazy about education there, the East Coast snobs. Her girl was studying at some Ivy League college, and her boy was at NYU medical school and had to study around the clock, too. Kathy complained that she wanted them to go out and have a life like other normal young people. I wished Alex and I had her problems. Also, she joked that with having two kids in college, she and her husband would have to exist on bread and water to make ends meet. I wonder whether an Ivy League school is more expensive than rehab? It probably is. But for college tuition, you pay by the year, and for a rehab, you pay by the month. If you stay in rehab for a year, it is definitely more than $40,000. Well, I would need to think about it.

Kathy called me with a brilliant idea. She offered to host Julia so that she could spend a month or two with her younger cousins while they were on summer vacation. I asked her whether she was sure and whether she realized the consequences.

She said, "If you are implying that my kids will be endangered by bad influences, I can tell you that, first of all, they are grownups, and I don't believe that Julia could teach them something bad. They are too mature compared to her, even though she is older. Secondly, if she drags them out to have some fun, I will only be happy. So don't worry and send her here immediately. I still owe you for our cousin Alexander, remember? Now is the time to pay you back."

Did I love our cousin Alexander more than ever at that moment!

Julia was not too thrilled about this idea and began listing the reasons against going. She said her New York cousins were two lunatics, she would be embarrassed to go out with them if they still dressed the way they did when they were teenagers, and she would be bored to death there without her friends. But, luckily for us, she had a fight with her boyfriend and wanted to leave for a while to teach him a lesson. Also, she was behind on her rent again, so it was a good excuse to put her stuff into storage, let her apartment go, and not pay rent for a month. And when she returned in a month or two…Oh well, who thinks so far ahead, anyway?

Off she went, and we did what we always did when our relationship was in a crisis, whether physically or emotionally: We took vacations to revive our romance. Alex had a very dependable young guy in his business then—Steven. He even planned to make him his partner. Alex had very strong technical skills but was limited in marketing, advertising, and public relations. Steve possessed all of those skills. He was a college dropout who did not like studying but liked action. He took the company to a whole new level. Together, they made a very effective team; one could not succeed without another. So, at that time, Alex could afford to leave his business in Steven's hands and take a couple weeks of vacation.

I did not see my old friends M&M too often anymore, and we grew apart. We still loved each other tremendously, but over the years, we became more conservative, Alex and I (not when it came to Julia, though), and they became more liberal. So when we met, we argued about everything. But if we avoided discussing any controversial issues, we got along just fine. Dangerous topics included politics, movies, books, philosophy, common friends, work, people's behavior, America, and life in general. So all that was left was the weather (no touching global warming, though), the latest fashions, and health problems.

The latter was becoming a more and more entertaining subject every year. The second I felt we were entering dangerous territory, I would say something like, "Maggie, do you have sleeping problems? How come every year we sleep worse and worse, and then we are tired all day long?" Another engrossing topic would always be weight gain: "I don't know about you, but no matter what I eat, I gain weight all the time." And the other party would always reply with, "Didn't you hear about the latest findings? If you eat more of…" And so we were safely out of the woods and actively involved with subject matter applicable to everyone but Alex. He still remained skinny.

We used to take vacations together, and when traveling, we complemented each other well. In an effort to relive the good old times, we agreed to take another trip together. We flew to Munich, rented a car, and drove through the Czech Republic, where Monie and Sigismund had a flat in Prague and were spending the summer. It was beautiful, it was educational, and it was delicious and fattening.

Sigismund took it very seriously when he had to tour Prague with new visitors. He imposed real terror on us; we would meet very early in the morning to see everything on his itinerary. He didn't leave anything to chance. Even before we came, he interviewed the tour guides to find the right ones for the city tour and the Jewish Quarter tour, and even then, he constantly corrected the guides during the tours. We ate *koleno* (pork knee) only at the places he approved; after eating, we would walk across the whole city just to have *polachenki* (blintzes) for desert at the place he deemed the best in the city. Then we would take a taxi to drink what he said was the best beer, one kind for the girls and another for the boys, and God forbid if we confused them. He even controlled what toilet we used after drinking the beer. Then he took us to the only store where he would allow us to buy the "right" garnets. Alex got so carried away by being so free and happy that he forced me to buy a very expensive set with the "right" garnets set in gold. He said it would be our vacation souvenir. I enjoyed being normal like other people; I had forgotten the feeling. For two weeks, I did not feel like an outcast. Alex was funny, smart, sexy, and intelligent, and he was always such delightful company. He was not himself when he had to adjust his brain to talk to Julia. Now he was being himself.

Finally, the time came to say good-bye to Monie and Sigismund. He was so exhausted after our whirlwind tour or Prague that he was coming down with something. But we saw, ate, and drank everything we had to, whether we liked it or not, and he was satisfied.

M&M, Alex, and I were headed north to Germany, but we had to stop for a day in Karlovy Vary because Sigismund wanted us to try the only plum strudel he would let us eat in the Czech Republic. He also told us what restaurant to go to for dinner. He even surprised us by calling the owner, who he knew, to check whether we came, whether we ordered the right food, and whether he gave us the right table so that we could watch the sunset while eating. As you are well aware of by now, he was taking fun very seriously. He left nothing to chance. After that we were allowed to leave the country.

Germany was not as delicious and fattening, but we had Sigismund's list of beer we had to drink when in Germany, so his spirit accompanied us.

We visited with Alex's old friends from his previous life who now lived in Germany. They picked us up at the hotel, and we went out to dinner with them and M&M.

We ate and danced and had an enjoyable evening. Alex was a good dancer. He was good at whatever he did. As for me, I am an average dancer. Sometimes, I would ask him to invite somebody else to dance, but he always refused, saying he only danced with his wife. I don't consider myself a jealous person, despite whatever Alex may think, but it was nice of him all the same.

Alex was ecstatic to catch up with his old friend David. He showed David and his wife, Tamara, the pictures he had brought with him for just that purpose: a few of Julia (of course), a few of our house, one showing us wearing a tuxedo and an evening gown (which was thoroughly scrutinized by Tamara), and last but not least, a few of his famous fiftieth birthday showing how many friends he had.

David was the type of man I used to like before I met Alex—bookish and unkempt. I would have never pictured him with a wife like Tamara, who had white hair, a white face, pale eyes, and white lips. All of her being was colorless. She had generously painted red lips, red cheeks, black eyes, and *very* black eyebrows on that blank slate of a face, and after talking to her for a few minutes, one could conclude that her brain was just as blank. She wore a skintight red décolleté sweater that showed her old, flabby bust, and all the rest was shiny gold: gold high heels, gold tights, a gold purse, and lots of gold jewelry. She was skinny and shapeless and dressed like a young girl. Her face was very old, and her makeup was overdone. In trying to look sexy, she only looked pathetic. She stood out in a crowd, and everybody stared at her, which she took as admiration.

I looked at the elegant, well-kept Maggie; then I remembered Monie, who was naturally beautiful and aristocratic, yet modest; and finally, my eyes moved back to Tamara. Pure harlequin.

I was reminded of that kind of faceless and classless Russian village girl.

I sound mean, I know. And, as you remember, I don't judge people by their appearance; therefore, I would never bother you or myself with all these details, if not for what happened next.

When the band started playing rock and roll, Tamara said, "Alex, let's remember the good old days." She grabbed Alex's hand and literally dragged him to the dance floor. The two of them started whipping out numbers as if they were professionals who had been dancing together for ages—they were awesome. When the band stopped, Alex and Tamara received a standing ovation from the other patrons in the restaurant because of how entertaining and exciting they were to watch.

Then a slow dance started, and Alex forced me to dance with him. So we danced, and they watched. When the music stopped, he pulled me closer and kissed my ear. Despite my apprehension about his public displays of affection, he always kissed me after each dance.

When we came back to our table, Tamara said, "Alex has changed his taste. He used to like *very* beautiful and *very* skinny girls."

I was crushed by her paltry comment after having been proud that I was in very good shape and looked my best that night.

Alex jumped to defend me. "I used to like beautiful girls, and now I like only one beautiful girl."

"That's what husbands always say," she continued. "Victoria, darling, how does it feel to have a gorgeous husband? Oh my, was he hot! Did women love him! Every girl was hitting on him. Always handsome, always impeccably dressed, and always fun. He had tons of women."

My evening was ruined. "They told me I was very hot, too." I replied. "It's too bad we didn't meet before so that he wouldn't have had to go through so many whores."

I was ashamed of myself for what I had just said. She brought out the worst in me.

"Tamara, were you one of them?" my faithful friend Maggie decided to help the situation.

When we returned to our hotel and were left alone, Alex was so scared that I was angry and hurt.

"Vika, don't listen to her! That bitch!" he said.

I couldn't help recalling Maggie's senseless interference. Usually, her spontaneous instincts were right.

"Alex, she sounded as if she were jealous. Did you have an affair with her?"

He hesitated for a moment. "I don't remember."

Sometimes men are so stupid when they are pressed to lie.

"You don't remember? I take that as a yes. So you slept with your good friend's wife?"

"She was not his wife at the time."

I wanted to laugh at this logical answer, but I hadn't decided yet whether I should let myself be upset about something that had happened more than twenty years prior.

"I wasn't crazy about her," he went on, "so I introduced her to him. He liked her better."

But why did we have to meet with them if something wasn't kosher?

"Can you remind me again why we had to see that clown tonight?"

205

"Because David was a very good friend of mine. I wanted to show him how phenomenal my life had become and the kind of woman I have for a wife."

"And what kind is that?"

"Very beautiful inside and outside. A very quality woman. I wanted him to see what kind of woman I finally found."

"Could you not convey this fiction to him over the phone?"

"Men don't discuss their wives over the phone. They can only briefly mention whether they are good or bad in bed."

"What do men usually discuss over the phone, then?"

"I don't know. Business, chicks."

I was speechless. I wasn't sure whether I hated or liked him being so frank and straightforward. We never talked about this kind of stuff before. I kept silent.

"Vika, listen, I was always faithful to my wife. And when I became wifeless, I did date women. I was looking for you. How could I know which one was you?"

The generosity of this statement took my breath away. And these were not just empty words. I would never expect him to master such an eloquent statement, so it was not just flattery; there were sincere feelings behind this sentiment.

"You dirty old playboy! Next time we go on vacation, I will make sure we meet with my ex-lovers."

"What lovers? I will kill you. Vika, are we OK? Can you smile for me, please? That's my girl!"

I decided to stop this nonsense. If that bitch's intention was to ruin the special bond we had, just for that reason alone I would not let her do it. He was relieved by my change of heart in not allowing myself to descend into a fit of jealous rage over his old romances. He pulled me close to him, and as he used to, he kissed me on the lips, which he did very seldom now. He then kissed my neck, and the earth moved under our feet just like it had years ago during our happiest of times.

Before falling into a contented sleep holding hands as we used to do, he said, "I love you, my darling. Don't you ever forget it."

"I love you more."

Life was as good as it used to be.

Oh, the luxury of being slightly jealous or making somebody jealous! Just as normal people do. We did not entertain such sweet extravagance in years. And the luxury of such arguments followed by the sweet and intoxicating reconciliations! Just as the young lovers do. We had been deprived of it for years.

Vacations do revive romance.

I am sure some young people will laugh at me at this point, but wait till you are in your forties, as I was then. Yes, I could still be in love, and I was. The more I knew that man, the more in love I became.

Alex called Kathy a few times, but I pretended not to notice. My body was in recuperation mode, or rather, in lifesaving mode. I felt almost as optimistic as I had years ago when I was a real optimist.

We flew home with the feeling that life was looking up. We believed everything would be resolved somehow. If only Julia settled down, the rest would fall into place. Because we are perfect for each other, we loved our life, we loved our work, and we shared the same values. How more perfect could it be? If only Julia took care of herself and Danny came home safe. I prayed to my grandma: "Please protect Danny. Please give Julia some common sense."

We had two happy weeks of vacation, plus we had two happy weeks after, until Kathy called.

"Hi, my dear. How are you?"

"Who cares! How are *you*?"

"Vika, if I told you that Julia is going home immediately, would you be upset with me for not keeping her for the whole six weeks as planned? Or would you be grateful for stealing one month of happiness from your nasty life?"

"Well, my dear, you hid the answer in your question. I always knew you were a very smart woman. How very unfortunate that it doesn't run in the whole family."

"You didn't answer my question."

"As you implied I should answer, I am very grateful for stealing a whole month of happiness from my nasty life. It was very generous of you. I mean it."

"Do you know who helped me to make this decision to cut her stay short? You."

"I would hate any person who helped you make such a decision, even if it was me."

"Remember the argument we had when you told me that one has to take care of oneself and one's family before one goes around trying to help other people?"

"Yes, I remember. You didn't agree with me."

"Vika, do you still believe it?"

"More than ever."

"All right, then. I have to protect my family. I have children, too, you know. I will bring her home tomorrow. Pick her up at the airport, would you? I will fly right back."

It sounded so severe that my optimism faded right away.

"Kathy, why are you flying with her?"

"Because I couldn't get the next-day nonstop flight, and I cannot promise that she will not disappear when she changes planes in Kansas City."

"That good, huh?"

Julia was coming back. It was all coming back.

❧

CHAPTER 29
FROM HEAVEN TO HELL IN ONE DAY

We picked Julia up from the airport, and she stayed with us for a couple of weeks. For the first few days, she was like a zombie, and then she started to sound and act more like herself, whining that we lived too far from where the action was. Supposedly, she was looking for a job. In two weeks, she moved in with her old boyfriend, Ben. We knew that spelled trouble, but she would not consider any other boring possibilities, like renting a tiny apartment or staying with us in our quiet suburb. No, not Julia. She was living on the Wilshire Corridor, and her beat-up car was being parked by a valet.

We lived our life hoping against hope. Julia would disappear for months and months. Alex threatened her again that she didn't have a father anymore, but she refused to be upset about it. Father schmather, who cared? To be honest, I have to admit that when she was sober, she adored him. They had a really special bond. They were not like father and daughter; they were like friends. (I am not sure whether it was a good thing. I believe in parental authority, but that is another subject.) But when she was even a little "warm" she became ruthless and did not care about anything but getting high.

Those months that followed were the worst ever. If we had established some control over her before, being with that guy changed everything. We had to deal with the two of them. He was her father now; we absolutely lost our leverage with her. She almost completely disappeared from our life.

Whenever Alex was able to reach her and talk to her, it was always about her car either being taken to the shop or taken from the shop or not being taken from the shop because she did not have money to pay for the repair. The number of accidents they had was unreal. A few times they went to the hospital. And they lost their apartment, of course. We had no idea where they lived. She would say that sometimes they stayed with their "friends" and other times at a motel.

Belka called. I recognized her number on the caller ID. How did she sense that I needed her? I called her back immediately.

"What did you want?"

"Hi, Victoria. I love you, too. What else is good?"

"Except you loving me, too? Let's see. Julia totaled another car. But don't despair—miraculously the insurance of the other party is paying for her car. They probably are too happy that she didn't kill their client. I don't know how it happens that she always gets away with all this crap, but what I do know is that one day he or she will kill somebody. I am so disappointed in this country."

"Finally. You always sound like an overly dedicated citizen to me."

"It's not funny what has been going on for a second year already! We are helpless, and we can do nothing. Everybody is literally sitting on the sidelines watching how this horror movie will end. They must do something about people in such a condition! They are walking or driving weapons of mass destruction. This country has to create some laws to isolate people in such condition until they get back to their senses— forcefully, if need be!"

"They cannot take them to prison for a crime they did not commit yet."

"So let's wait until they commit it. How logical. But guess what? When it finally happens, a good lawyer will tell the story of a hard childhood or an unhappy love, and they are back on the streets in no time to endanger themselves and others. They must establish prisons for drug addicts. OK, don't call them prisons; call them high-security rehabs. They have to be held there against their will if they do not pass the drug test."

"It sounds too severe. Also, can you imagine how many people would have to be held there? Who would pay for it?"

"Do you know how much it costs everybody when a person is on drugs? Hospitals nonstop, police nonstop, rehabilitation programs, disability insurance, et cetera. Also, all parents would be happy to pay to put their children into prison when they are in that condition. It sounds unreal, but everything is unreal when drugs are concerned. It is like this: prison or morgue. I bet you that parents who have gone through what we are going through—or through even worse, God forbid—will tell you that they would gladly pay to imprison their son or daughter. Only then can the parents take a breath. Alex is not living. He is doing what he is supposed to do, but all he can think about is whether she is still alive today or not. We live in a vacuum because all the life has been sucked from our home. Our marriage…Belka, here I am again—"

"No, no, no, it's different this time. As soon as it ends this way or the other, you will have your Alex back. He is your man."

"This way or the other…If it ends the other way, I will have no Alex. Even if he is physically alive, he will be dead. I don't want a dead life. That is it. That's exactly what we have now—a dead life."

"Vika, can you imagine how much easier it would be if we were religious? They deprived us of that when we were growing up, too. But I'll tell you something, and you have to believe me that I mean it, and I'm not just trying to comfort you. There *is* faith, even though we are very materialistic, all of us who came from that sick country. So have faith. You don't know what will happen. It might all end well."

"Belka, I don't see how. But believe it or not, I do believe in God now. I don't necessarily believe in any particular religion yet, but there is supposed to be a universal mind. Oh well, that is too big a talk for now. We'll postpone it until happier times."

"How is Alex? Does he take it out on you?"

"No, not at all. Quite the opposite. The angrier he is with her, the warmer he is with me, and vice versa. It was always like that. When she is all right, according to his standards, he is very rough with me for my not praising her. When he is like he is now, loving and warm, I can do anything for him—anything. Like give him my kidney, for example. And he has my heart already."

"Ha-ha, how funny. You used to be funnier. Did you hear from Danny?"

Another ping to my heart—ouch, that hurt.

"He is fine by comparison…He is planning to come home. I really hold my breath. I want to touch him. Is he real? I don't remember."

"What happened to your optimism and sense of humor? He is a winner, did you forget? Whatever he decides to do in life, he is always a winner."

"Whatever you say."

I hung up, and then I remembered that I did not ask Belka how she was doing. But that's fine. Belka would understand; she always had.

On Julia's birthday in November, Alex started calling her, desperate to wish her a happy birthday. For a while, he had been pretending that he didn't want to know about her anymore, but her birthday was an excuse. He called and called. And then he called Ben's cell and left a message. I didn't even know he had his number.

The next day, Ben called him back, which was a shocker; we did not count on it. He informed us that Julia had spent the day in the hospital. They were celebrating her birthday with some "friends," and she overdosed. Ben called the paramedics, who were barely able to revive her, but she was feeling better. Alex was shattered. He could not get over the fact that she almost died on her birthday. Somehow it sounded too ironic. He said again and again, "Just think of it, her birthday could have been her death day."

I remembered my talk with Belka.

"Alex, would you pay for Julia to be shut up in prison right now?"

"Any money. I would hold her there for a year or more. Maybe she would sober up. Maybe they would teach her a lesson. Maybe it would be so horrible that she would think twice when she wants to snort something next time."

Wow, this coming from mellow Alex…

It gave me an idea.

"Let's call the police and tell them that we know somebody who is doing drugs right now and give them their address—like an anonymous tip. Ben told you what motel they are staying at now."

"We discussed this already, remember? They will only arrest you if they catch you selling drugs—or if you killed somebody."

America! Help! You are such a smart, kind, and considerate country, but maybe you are too kind, too considerate, and not too pragmatic. Insane people are supposed to be forcefully put into institutions, and drug addicts are supposed to be forcefully put into closed rehabs! There were probably some instances of abuse when they mistakenly held normal people as insane. But to avoid a few instances, they would rather wait until it ends tragically for thousands or hundreds of thousands. How many were on drugs at some point in their lives? How many others were affected? Something is very wrong with this picture.

CHAPTER 30
THANKSGIVING AND NEW YEAR'S

Life continued—or more accurately, limped—on. We had our Thanksgiving at Greg's, as usual. Nelly's turkey was exceptional, as usual. Danny came back just in time to see the family at Thanksgiving. We were not used to having him around, and the first half hour or so felt awkward, as he was not aware of anything that was going on in our lives. But then we ate and drank and became easy again. Danny always had a special bond with Greg. He tended to have more respect for men, which is typical Russian chauvinism. Just joking. He also had a very good relationship with Alex. But now he was staying with us for a few weeks, and I felt that there was some tension. Alex did not like having anybody living with us, which did not apply to Julia, of course. It made me very angry, but I had no fight left in me. Danny, being difficult, as usual, did not help the situation. I just tried to please everybody and went out of my way to make my men happy. Danny was moving to an apartment he had found in early December, so they would both be just fine.

To us Russians, New Year's is the biggest holiday of the year. Since any religion was outlawed in the Soviet Union, we had no concept of Christmas, Hanukkah, Easter, etc. We celebrated Communist holidays and New Year's. New Year's was a new beginning, and it was the only spiritual thing we could have. It was the anticipation of something new and hopefully happy. I had no idea whatsoever that New Year's had any relation to anything religious. We put out a Christmas tree to celebrate New Year's, which was called the "New Year's pine tree." We exchanged gifts and stayed up until the dawn celebrating. It was big. It was huge. There is a saying that the way you meet the New Year will be the way you spend the year, and if you make a wish when the clock strikes midnight, it will come true. That's how it was in Russia.

So, even now, we make sure we have a good plan to spend New Year's Eve. That year, we rang in the New Year at our friends' house, complete with costumes, dancing, eating, drinking, and plenty of laughter. I made my requisite phone calls to my parents and Danny (Greg and Nelly were there with us) to wish them a happy and healthy New Year at ten minutes to midnight, and Alex called Julia a few times on her cell phone, hoping to say happy New Year to her and hear her voice on New Year's Eve. Unable to reach her, he left her a few messages wishing her a happy New Year. When our West Coast rerun of the Times Square countdown indicated midnight, champagne bottles began popping, and we started screaming and cheering. In Russia, it is a very important custom to kiss who is most important to you right when the clock is chiming; I think the same is true here. Alex drank his champagne, probably made a daring wish related to Julia, hugged and kissed me, and whispered in my ear, "Happy New Year, my love. It was the worst year of my life. I am so glad it is over." And I saw tears in his eyes.

Oh Alex, my Alex. I will never let you down. We are one.

CHAPTER 31

I AM ILL

It was a beautiful Sunday morning in the spring, and we invited two other couples over to spend the day together. We had planned to go hiking, but I did not feel well, so we decided to have breakfast on the lake and enjoy the scenery instead. I love going out for breakfast the best; it is even more festive than dinner. The mountains were still the vibrant green of spring's renewal, which would eventually fade to yellow in the coming months. Our lake and surroundings are always so spectacular and tranquil—it takes your breath away.

When we returned home, I got out of our friends' car and promptly fainted, which, of course, created a big fuss. They carried me inside, and I came back from wherever I was. It was so embarrassing that I wanted to cry—what a hostess. Covered in cold perspiration, I was overcome with nausea, and the pain in my chest and stomach were unrelenting. I was sure I had eaten something bad. I tried to get up but could not. Alex and our friends conducted a quick opinion poll, and the overwhelming majority decided it was necessary to take me to the hospital.

When we arrived at the emergency room, I was immediately given oxygen, hooked up to an ECG, and plugged into an IV. In addition, they performed tons of tests, and I could not wait to see the bill. I kept insisting that I just had indigestion or a stomach flu. Ignoring my appeals, they transferred me to the ICU. They sedated me and wheeled me somewhere to perform the cardiac angiogram, after which I underwent angioplasty and stent placement. In my semiconscious state, I wondered whether that young-looking Asian boy next to me could possibly be the doctor. He was barely out of kindergarten, appearing much younger than my Danny. Were they sending medical students to practice their skills on Sundays so that the real doctors could rest? After they were done with me and I was moved to the room, he came to visit. Indeed, he was a doctor. He assured me that the procedure was very successful and that they were able to remove some pieces of clots from the artery and place three stents. I really had a problem this time. But, according to him, it was not a big deal, as we were able to do everything in a timely manner. He warned me that I had to start exercising *again* soon, as if I had been exercising even when I was still healthy. Later, other cardiologists who reviewed my case confirmed that that adolescent had done a superb job and that I was very lucky. God bless him; his mama should be very proud of him.

I spent three days in the hospital, and Alex was there with me every second of every day. He held my bedpan, washed me with wet towels, held my head when I vomited, and combed my hair. I forbade him to tell anybody of my hospitalization, as I did not want any calls or visitors. Only Greg came once because he did not care what I said. When he came, Alex went home for an hour to take a shower and a nap. It was then that Greg told me that Julia was in the hospital again and had called Alex to visit her. Alex told Julia that he had other priorities now, as his wife was very sick and he had to be with her, so she would have to do without him. Then Greg related Alex's call to Danny in which he told him that if he (Alex) ever saw his (Danny's) mother cry, he (Danny) would not be welcome in our house anymore. This last news would have broken my heart if it hadn't been broken already by the heart attack that was starting when they brought me to the hospital. So I just hoped that Danny would forgive us. When he came to visit, it looked as if this story was not true; he was warm and concerned. Or maybe shockotherapy worked again?

When I was discharged, I stayed home for a few weeks. I asked Alex not to speak the name *Julia* until I had completely recovered. For the first time in my life, I was doing nothing, and I liked it a lot. It occurred to me that I am probably a very lazy person by nature but just never had the chance to be lazy. And thanks a lot for that.

Upon my return to work, there were so many balloons and flowers waiting for me that they didn't all fit in my cubicle. I was so touched. I had strictly prohibited everyone from visiting or sending flowers or anything of the kind, but my coworkers had not forgotten about me. I wanted to kiss those dear people and those dear walls again.

The first Wednesday after I came home, Danny came over for dinner. I was not well enough to cook yet, so he brought food and a movie we had wanted to see. We had a wonderful time, the three of us, just eating and watching the movie together. It was the best remedy I could have asked for. Starting that week, Danny came for dinner every Wednesday. I knew I had to be ready and save the evening for him. Small talk, light food, and a light-hearted movie—once a week, we all came together and shunned the outside world with its important problems and took pleasure in enjoying these unimportant things. Although, what could be more important than reviving a connection with my Danny? Danny and I were finally getting to know each other again. I used to admire Dale Carnegie, whose advice imparts that if you want your kids to visit, make it a pleasure, not a chore.

I eventually learned that Alex and Danny agreed on starting this tradition when I was in the hospital. It was the best gift Alex could have ever given me.

Sometimes Danny would get a bit edgy; he was still impatient with me at times. But with Alex around, he would quickly remember the promise he had given to him.

We all went back to our normal—meaning abnormal—life. I was afraid people around me would see me as a handicap, so I did everything in my power not to remind others about it, and we all almost forgot about it.

I also quit smoking again—hopefully for good this time. Alex promised to quit smoking, too.

PART 6

BECOMING STRANGERS

CHAPTER 32
VIP RESORT BY THE OCEAN

In late summer, a staff member from the Rehab by the Ocean called on Julia's behalf to inquire whether we were willing to pay for her to spend a few months there. When she told us how much it was, I thought she had misspoken and asked whether it was per month or per year.

Alex was so happy that we had heard from Julia that I could not fail him. I told him that we would send a check for the first month right away. He said that he would agree to spend this kind of money *only* if I insisted. I said I insisted, and boy was he happy! With Julia under control for a month, he was so relieved to be able to sleep through the night without constant worry. Alex called her every evening to reason with her and brainwash her for hours. She listened contentedly, giving him hope. He was glowing; he was as proud of her as if she had just received a Nobel Prize, or at least graduated from a medical school, which is a more prosperous prospect, I think. When asked how we were doing, he would reply that everything was all right, that Julia was sick and in a very fancy hospital at the moment, but soon she would be out and would start looking for a job and an apartment.

Julia's periodic updates on her stay there continuously impressed him.

"Vika, did you hear it? Julia is saying that famous Danny Galinny is a patient there as well! And you will never guess who was just discharged—Sonia Berman! Can you believe it? But wait until you hear who Julia's sponsor is going to be—the Freddie Price himself! Vika, Julia is saying hi to you. Sweetie, Vika is saying hi to you, too. Talk to you tomorrow."

"Alex, you insult my intelligence."

"Why not give a girl a second chance?"

"Alex, I thought you were good at mathematics. This is a problem for a first grader—how many times can you give somebody a *second* chance?"

"I thought you would be happy for me."

Did I really marry this primitive and shallow person? I would be very happy for him, and for myself, but there was nothing to be happy for yet. And the main thing was his constant bragging about all of this.

He went to visit her that Sunday, and when he came back, he told me how much he liked the place. Allegedly, there were many famous people, but Julia was absolutely the prettiest there and looked just stunning. She claimed that somebody had taken an interest in her and promised to make a portfolio with her pictures to help her become a movie star. He was actually serious as he delivered these unconceivable tales. It was as if nothing bad had happened during the last few years. He discounted all the horror I had gone through. All of that was dismissed, my heart attack was dismissed, and all of a sudden, I was requested to admire her and acknowledge her success. I even suspected that he thought I might be jealous of what was happening to her; I would never have such an adorable sponsor.

Kathy called; he answered the phone.

"Things are just great. Julia finally did the right thing. She is in a very famous rehab by the ocean. There are only celebrities there because you cannot imagine how much it costs. You will not believe what people have been there over the years. It's a very exclusive place, with very exclusive people. And Freddie Price himself will be her sponsor! She will even be invited to attend some parties at their home! What? Well, I am not quite sure what *sponsor* means, but he will probably be taking care of her or mentoring her—something really good and important. How are your kids, my little sis? I hope they are doing great, too. Oh, no way! Nicole is engaged? Congrats! Who is the boy? You're kidding me, the same one we saw when we were there five years ago? She is really loyal. And Mark is moving to Arizona? Why? Can't he find any place closer to do his residency? But, anyway, congratulations! Although, it is better when they are close to you. Kind of under control, if you know what I mean. Yep, Vika is great, too. Sure, here she is."

"Hello, Kathy. You know everything already. I have little to add."

"Are you thinking what I'm thinking?"

"I guess so."

"You know, I called to offer some support and maybe some money to help with rehab, but I am afraid I cannot afford such a famous sponsor. My brother's speech made me sick. Beggars cannot be choosers."

"Don't worry about it. You know I don't expect other people to take care of our problems."

"I feel really bad for you, dear."

I could not continue the conversation because Alex was listening.

"All right, then. I am very happy for your kids. And don't worry, Mark is a man who can live without your control."

When I hung up, Alex said, "Sometimes Kathy can be very stuck-up. She is so proud of her children, as if they had made something of themselves already. Who knows what life has in store for them?"

"Let's hope that it's only the best." I was revolted by his remark.

"She has to be happy for me that, for once, everything is working out. She could even help with my payments. Family has to help in a crisis."

"Alex, if you told her that Julia is at some prison camp for drug addicts and starving there, Kathy would give her last penny. But, no, Julia had to find the most expensive place on earth, and you even go around boasting about it. Beggars cannot be choosers." What a copycat I was.

"My daughter is not a beggar!"

"No, she is not. Wouldn't that be nice! She is a demander. Had she been forced to work for years to collect the money to pay for that rehab, she would probably prefer some cheaper prison camp for drug addicts. And maybe then it would finally help her and teach her something."

He did not answer, but I did not like the look in his eyes.

He did not talk to me for three weeks. Alex was a very patient and agreeable person in everyday life because he didn't know how to quarrel. But when he finally submitted to an altercation, he absolutely didn't know how to make peace and get back to normal again. He was not forgiving. So we fought very few times in our fifteen years together. This time it was very severe. He could not get over the fact that I put my principles before him. How could I explain to him that I would do anything for him, as I knew he would for me? But I could not call black, white, and I could not call wrong, right—even for him.

Nothing could make me more heartbroken than Alex not talking to me. When I had arguments with Danny, it was Alex who comforted me. And who would comfort me now? I just did not know how to deal with it.

Max was in a bad car accident, and I was spending nearly every other night at the hospital trying to help Maggie. At least I did not have to be home every evening to breathe that heavy air of my husband's anger.

Julia spent exactly three weeks at that place, at which time she was involuntarily discharged for breaking the rules. I did not ask Alex for details, because first of all, he still wasn't speaking to me, and secondly, I did not want to hear, once again, how mean people could be and how unlucky this poor, trusting, beautiful girl was.

Julia professed that she was starting a new life. Alex coldly asked me if I minded that Julia would live with us for a short time since she was a "changed" person now—after just three weeks of fame. Did he forget that I almost died just recently? Thank goodness she refused because we lived too far from the city center where celebrities belong. She went to live with some friends. Ben was at some other rehab at the time, and she was waiting for him to become a "changed" person, too, so they could start living together again. But at least asking this question forced Alex to start talking to me again.

In a few weeks, Kathy called back to check on us. While Alex was talking to her, I picked up the second phone and said, "Kathy, I ran across a very interesting piece of literature. I want to read it to you."

"Peace of literature? That's what we need now the most. Do I have to listen to it, too?" Alex sounded irritated.

"Alex, we cannot enjoy literature anymore? Did she deprive me of that, too? Please, do me this favor. It will take two minutes. Here it is."

THE PREACHMENT ABOUT A GOOD MOTHER, A BAD MOTHER, AND UNCONDITIONAL LOVE

There was a young widow. She worked hard to provide for her only son. He was everything she had, and she lived for him. He adored his mother, as all little sons do.

She would sit by his bed and sing that old song[6] to him:

> *You and me against the world*
> *Sometimes it feels like you and me against the world*
> *When all the others turn their back and walk away*
> *You can count on me to stay.*

Once, when he was a teenager, he came home smelling of alcohol. He said that he had had a few beers with the boys and that he was driving home when he accidentally hit another car. He did not stop to see the damage because he was afraid that those people would call the police, and the police would find out that he was drinking and driving. His car was damaged. He begged his mother to help him fix the car so that it did not have signs of an accident.

The mother said that she was not going to cover his drunk driving, and if he didn't call the police and report the hit-and-run himself, she would.

He picked up the phone and called the police. Then he looked at her with such hatred and said, "What ever happened to 'you and me against the world'?"

She said, "It is just a song. But in real life, the time will come when you have to learn how to act as a man when it is only you against the world."

He was not eighteen yet, so he got his driver's license suspended for a year and one year of community service. She drove him to work every morning now, and every morning when leaving her car, he would say, "It is your doing. You ruined my life. I hate you." Every weekend when he had to get up early and go to

---

6   "You and Me Against the World" by Kenny Ascher and Paul Williams

sweep the streets, he would say, "It is your fault. I hate you. You are not a mother."

He could not wait to get out and go to college. She worked two jobs and paid as much as she could afford, and he took a loan for the rest. He did not call too often, and when she would visit, he could not wait for her to leave.

He made it just fine. He became any mother's dream. She was proud to know him. When she met him at some events, she was so joyous to watch people admiring him. But it was obvious that he was not too fond of her. To his friends, he was always saying, "I hate my mother. She is an old, pathetic loser."

He became very successful, married, and had his own kids. When his children became teenagers, he came to his mother and said, "Now, having my own kids, I probably have to thank you for turning me in at the time. But my love for you is lost forever. I hated you for so long that I am used to it now, and it is very unfortunate."

When he left, she exclaimed, "Oh dear God, please allow me to relive everything. I want my son back. Please perform a miracle!"

And God answered, "All right. I will give you this unique opportunity to turn back time."

So she found herself a young widow again. Her teenage son came home, and he smelled of alcohol. He said that he had had a few beers with the boys and that he was driving home when he accidentally hit another car. He did not stop to see the damage because he was afraid that the people would call the police, and the police would find out that he was driving under the influence. His car was damaged. He begged his mother to help him fix the car so that it did not have signs of the accident.

The next morning, his mother took his car to a mechanic she knew and paid a lot of money to have it fixed. She told the mechanic that she hit the car, and he asked her why she didn't want to call her insurance company so that they would pay.

"That's what insurance is for," he said.

She had to lie to him. "I am late with my payment, so I don't think the insurance company will pay."

The car was fixed, and when the police came knocking on the door asking whether anybody knew anything about that hit-and-run collision, she was so glad that she had fixed the car and there were no witnesses. Her son was very scared and very thankful.

He said, "Mom, you are the best mother in the world and my best friend. I love you so much. You saved me."

And she replied, "That's what mothers do. They love their children unconditionally."

Then he started to drink more often, and every time he could not go to work, she would call his boss and make up some story. Because that's what good mothers do. She saved money and bought him a used SUV because she was afraid that, since he was drinking and driving, he could be injured if he collided with another car.

Finally, he got into a big accident and was admitted to the hospital. The person in the small sedan was killed. He was detained, and she asked all of the people she knew to lend her money to pay his bail while the investigation was going on. But she could not get so much money together, and he stayed in prison.

The night before the court date he wrote her a letter:

> *Dear mother, I want you to know how much I appreciate everything you've done for me and how much I love you. I feel like the two of us are against the whole world. I have no friends and no family, just you. No matter what happens tomorrow, I hope you will be comforted by knowing that I love you more than anything else in the world.*
>
> *Your unfortunate son*

She dropped to her knees and exclaimed, "Oh God, please allow me to take my first life back!"

God said, "All right, I can give it back to you. But you will lose your son's love."

"I'll take it."

When I finished, Alex said, "Did you just make that up to torture me?"

On the other line, Kathy said, "Vika, did you write this? It is very good! Have you ever considered writing?"

"No, she considers preaching. She is a saint and preaching all the time. Vika, can you tell me in simple language what the hell is it that you want from me?"

"I want closure. I want us to sit together—Julia, you, and I. I want us to acknowledge what we have gone through for years and call it exactly what it was. I want Julia to say what she thinks has been happening for the last few years, and then we close the chapter. We cannot go on without closure."

"I don't understand a word of what you've just said. I should have met somebody simpler and less sophisticated. Why don't you just be sad for me when I'm sad and happy for me when I'm happy? Why can't it be simple?"

"Remember the Russian proverb 'They beat you and don't let you cry'? All right, Alex, I will try to be simple."

Poor Kathy said, "All right, kids, I am glad you have finally agreed on something. Talk to you soon."

We went on with our lives for the sake of routine. It was not festive or exciting or full of tenderness anymore. We became two strangers.

∾

CHAPTER 33
POINT OF NO RETURN

A few months later, we had some friends visiting from Moscow. I decided to take a day off and show them something they had not seen yet. There are so many of our friends here that there was hardly anything else to show them. I took them to one of our beautiful botanical gardens and then to my favorite small museum in Los Angeles. As it was a weekday, we had the museum to ourselves. I was enjoying the serene atmosphere when my cell phone rang; I ran to the vestibule to take the call. I was sure it was Alex because we planned to meet him for dinner.

But, no, it was Julia. I had not heard her voice in months. She anxiously needed to talk to me because she was in detox at the hospital again and was being discharged from there. She was supposed to go live in a sober living home. This was one more thing I had to learn; I had never heard this term and had no idea what it meant. She proclaimed that she was not going there—period. It was for junkies, according to her, but she could stop doing drugs any minute she decided to, unlike other addicts, and therefore, she didn't need any sober living crap. She insisted that she move in with us until she felt strong enough to live on her own. She had called her father, but he couldn't make that decision without my consent, so she had to call me.

There I was, sitting in the vestibule of my favorite museum, ready to go shopping in my favorite city, and then to dinner with my friends and my favorite man, and in one quick moment everything changed. Nothing mattered anymore. Everything was the same, but nothing felt the same. The same paintings looked so insignificant, shopping seemed so stupid, and dinner, with all its frivolous conversation, felt so unimportant. All that really mattered were drugs, sober living, drug tests, and hiding medicine, wine, and money.

I know what drugs do. They break down the logic of your life, and of everybody's life, because they affect the mind, and the mind is the center of the universe. That's why I felt so cornered. In my world, reason and common sense rule. But when drugs are involved, there is no logic, no common sense, nor any other rules of life that can be applied. Under normal circumstances, I would unquestionably back up my husband's daughter who never had a normal mother. Suppose she were driving to her bar exam to become a lawyer and got into a car accident and broke her leg. I would push her wheelchair until she recuperated; I would nurture her until she got better. I would do it for anybody, for any responsible, self-sufficient human being, when this responsible, self-sufficient human being was *temporarily* not self-sufficient. But this creature, these drugs—everything in my perception of life was upside down. And I did not want it to be upside down. Ever since I was born, I have worked hard to put it in order. All these thoughts rushed through my mind in a matter of seconds.

"No."

She was so sure that she had not left us a choice that she did not believe me. "Excuse me?"

"You asked me something, and my answer is no."

"It can't be! Papa has been calling me like every day for months begging me to get back to a normal life. And now, when I am like on the way back and when everyone must help me with this, you say no?"

"I say no, and if your father says yes and kicks me out of my house, so be it."

"You know he will not kick you out, but you will break his heart, and you will be responsible for his heart attack!"

"That is rich! Let's put it this way, I am sure that if professional people say that you must go live in a sober living facility at this stage of your…um…um…disease, then it is probably the only right solution. So let's pretend I say no for your sake. That's going to be our official version. And, baby, if anybody is supposed to get a heart attack because of you, it is more logical that it should be your father rather than me." I wondered whether she knew about my heart attack. Probably not. She had been out of this world at the time.

I hung up, only to find my friends standing next to me, listening to the entire conversation. One of the ladies, a judge in Moscow, caught me off guard when she said, "You just did the right thing. I know these people. They will ruin their own life no matter what you do, and they will ruin yours if you let them."

They do have drug addicts now after all. They had definitely become closer to Europe since I left there.

I did not feel like going out anymore. I called Alex and told him that we were coming home for dinner. I was so glad we had visitors that evening because I was afraid to face him alone.

When he saw me, he said, "I know what happened, and I am glad you said no. I have absolutely no more energy to go through everything again."

Go figure. He probably wanted to say no to her himself but hoped that it would be me so that he would be the "good cop" and I would be the "bad cop." Just as well.

So she went to live in sober living homes on and off. She was supposed to pass periodic drug tests, which I think were not always successful. Sometimes she would call and tell us that she was living with some friends, so she would be out of touch for a while. Then she called and told us that she was moving out of state to attend some sobering community. We never knew what to believe because of her habitual lies. I asked Alex not to fill me in anymore because, unlike him, I didn't buy that crap. As a result, I could hear him lowering his voice and chatting on the phone for hours. If I had not known it was Julia, I would have thought he was talking to a lover—that's how intimate and gentle his voice was. He pleaded with her to be a good girl, seriously discussing what she had to wear for her next job interview. Once or twice, he briefly shared the latest news with me. She was living in a sober living home again, and he was very hopeful. Had he not learned anything? Did he have severe ADD, too? It was the same cycle: promises, hope, broken promises, and broken hearts.

When Kathy called, he could then open his mouth to a willing listener.

"Kathy, she is fine. But she hates it there, of course. The conditions are not very good, but at least she has to take drug tests regularly and it consoles me. She is not getting along with her roommate, who is some junkie. But what can I do? You know Vika. She wants to stay out of it now. I wish I could just do the same. What do you mean I should? No, I can't! It's easy for you to say. You should've gotten a kid like that, and then you would know. You are just lucky that your children are different. Julia needs support this time. Everything is complicated by the fact that she has a very nasty manager there who doesn't like Julia."

At this point of my eavesdropping, I knew what was coming. Knowing me well enough by now to predict what my reaction would be, he spoke in hushed tones.

"You know, they always hate her because she is pretty, dresses very nicely, and drives a fancy car. She is on this government program, you know, and she is eligible to attend certain schools to learn a profession. She applied for makeup designer school. They will have to find her a job afterward. She wants to be a makeup artist and work in Hollywood. They told her, at that college, she will be working for the Oscars, Emmy Awards, and stuff like that. She has huge makeup cases for her projects at school. She is doing very well, and her teachers praise her all the time. So you understand that she has to have a reliable car. In the last accident she had, when she was DUI, her car was totaled and so was the other car. She and that boy she hit were in the hospital with their injuries. Her insurance will have to pay for the car, so I recommended that she consider a bigger car because you know the way kids drive—it's crazy. Plus, she needs room to put all those cases for the college. All that being taken in consideration, Ben helped her find a very decent used Mercedes SUV 420. I would prefer for her to have something less flashy, because knowing human nature, it aggravates the manager at sober living. It's just a strong car to protect a fragile girl—what's the big deal about it?"

Alex continued talking to Julia every day; he enjoyed the good news from the fantasy world she was living in. Then her tone changed. She had been looking for a job as a makeup designer for a whole month, and—surprise, surprise—they were not exactly lining up to grab her. The Oscars came and went without Julia. She was very upset that, after her being in the program, nobody fulfilled his or her duty of giving her special treatment in life. Alex explained to her that looking for a job is a job in itself, and eventually, everything would work out in her favor. He encouraged her to not give up, reminding her that nothing is easy in life. He was thirty-plus years late in teaching this to her.

A month later, Alex planned for both of us to have breakfast with Julia because he wanted me to see for myself how well she was doing. We met at the café on Melrose Street, where Julia arrived in the beautiful, huge Mercedes; she looked stunning and was dressed like a model. Very glad to see us, she dragged us to her car to show us the cases of makeup.

We ended up having yearly lunch, which prompted Julia to suggest drinks.

"Let's order some wine to celebrate our meeting at last."

My heart stopped. "Can you have wine? I thought you were on a program. I heard you recently celebrated three months of sobriety."

"I decided to quit AA. I'm too busy now to go there all the time. I don't need that persistent brainwashing. So I'm not on a program anymore, and therefore, I can drink wine. You cannot drink wine only if you are on a program."

That was really logical. I looked at Alex, but he obviously did not get it. Was he that slow?

Despite the portfolio she showed us with pictures of her impressive work, she was still looking for a job. Alex swelled with pride.

When she left, he said, "Well, what do you say?"

"I say you don't drive a Mercedes when you live in a sober living home and attend a college at other people's expense."

"You're just jealous that she drives a Mercedes and you don't."

"If this is how you read me after knowing me for the past fifteen years, I have nothing else to add. I can't see how it can go on like this any longer."

"So when everything was going terribly wrong, you were there supporting me, facing problems with me, and solving them. Now, when she is finally becoming somebody, and we can at last live our life, you are telling me that you cannot take it anymore? Women. Who can understand you?"

POINT OF NO RETURN

"Alex, define 'becoming somebody.' Does driving a Mercedes mean becoming somebody? Why are you applying rules to her that you don't apply to yourself or other people? Do you know how damaging this boundless indulgence of yours is to her?"

"I don't understand a word you're saying. You lecture and lecture all the time. Why do you think that you always know better? Why don't you speak plainly and tell me what the heck it is that you want?"

"I am speaking very plainly. I cannot adjust my speech so that you, or even Julia, can understand. Isn't it abundantly clear that you don't park a Mercedes next to a sober living home?"

"Says who?"

"Says any decent person. And until you explain that to her, she will continue having problems with everybody, and not because she is beautiful. Alex, now you're thinking that I'm jealous of both her beauty and her Mercedes. And for the first time in our life together, I don't care what you think of me, and it scares the hell out of me."

"What do you want from me? Is it my business what she drives? Is it yours? As long as she doesn't do drugs, nothing else matters!"

"Does that apply to the rest of humanity? If Danny doesn't do drugs, then he can have a free ride in everything he wants?"

"Danny has a mother, a father, an uncle, a grandma, and a grandpa. Poor Julia has only me, and never ever will I abandon her."

"Julia has a mother, a father, an aunt, and grandparents, too!"

"Where are all of them? Nobody knows where her mother is. Her aunt doesn't give a crap about her. And her grandparents are in another country. And Danny's family is all here."

"So kill them all to be fair. If all of your family was so dysfunctional, you had no right getting involved with a normal woman with normal values. I am sick and tired of this ongoing drug extravaganza! I cannot imagine my life without you—the you that you were before. Everything changed and shifted. I would give up *anything* for you, but not what makes me, me. I will not call evil, godly—even for you."

"Victoria, I went through one divorce already, and it was very painful because of the child, but I survived. I am sure that the second time will be much easier."

On that very sunny morning, as we sat outside of that cozy café on Melrose Street, the earth did not open her mouth and swallow us up when he said it.

ॐ

PART 7

THE END OF THE HAPPY END

CHAPTER 34
NEXT YEAR

Some material things had to be taken care of, namely signing the divorce papers, continuing to go to work, putting our house (our baby) on the market, packing, and looking for an apartment. So, to survive, I used the old tactics. I tried to pretend that I went into hibernation again. I did everything required of me while on autopilot. Alex and I tried to see each other as little as possible while packing and selling the house. The amount of stuff we had accumulated during our fifteen years together was unbelievable! Alex always loved to throw things away, but now he went into a demolishing rage. He threw away things we used to treasure, everything that meant something to us as a couple. There were bags full of pictures and CDs and books as well as my gowns and his tuxedo, the ones we wore so proudly when going to our friends' children's weddings—"Mr. and Mrs. Lansky have arrived!" I saw him putting that memorable wall calendar with his fiftieth birthday photos aside at first, but then he tore it apart and threw it into the garbage, too.

When he saw the amount of things we had, all the china and sheets and vases and pots, everything we bought for life and to use when we were very old and still in love, he went berserk. He was ridding himself of our togetherness; he was smashing it all and putting it in garbage containers. It was his way of releasing anxiety, and I was happy that he figured out how to deal with it because I worried about him terribly. I knew from my previous experience that it takes years to get your husband out of your system and stop feeling responsible for his well-being.

I went through all my files and notebooks; I did not want to lose any important stuff like Danny's Who's Who certificate or his graduation pictures or my first divorce papers or my second marriage certificate. I'm sorry, Grandma, I failed you again. In our family, people don't get divorced—even once. But I did what you told me to do: I did not sell out and sacrifice my values because that would have killed me. I knew that if I did not relieve myself of that nauseating terror that accompanied my life with my beloved Alex, I would die. It still remained to be seen whether I would not die without him.

Wherever I looked—any paper, notebook, address book, or old purse—I had Julia's constantly changing phone numbers and addresses. There were her doctors' numbers, her friends' numbers, hospitals and rehabs, mental health institutions, and her boyfriends. I could trace her roaming for the fifteen years that I had known her. Nobody could have so many phone numbers and addresses. Did Alex realize how much of this was my work? All of it. All these notes were toxic, and it was exiting my life.

When Alex spent a day at home packing, I stayed with M&M. Somehow it was easier than being at Nelly's. I did not want her prying into the details of my private life in order to help me make the right decisions. Nelly was upset with me because of that and called me "Victoria's Secret." I had hurt her! Somehow everything was always about Nelly, even when it was about you.

Then Steven from Alvy Electric called.

"Vika, how are you doing? Don't answer. I know. Listen, we have some business to discuss with you. I am planning to hire a lawyer to deal with all of this."

"And how does that concern me?"

"This is the situation. I paid money to buy a piece of the ownership. You and Alex started the company together, and now you are divorcing. You will claim your share, I am sure. There are not many assets in the company yet, but we have potential. I want to protect myself and the company. So the reason I'm calling is to ask what you want to do about it."

"I absolutely don't plan to claim anything. It's Alex's whole life now. He worked his butt off for it. I would never harm him."

"Vika, this is what you say today. Ten years from now—"

"Steven," I interrupted him, "don't waste my time and yours. And don't waste Alex's money on lawyers. I'm sure you have the papers all ready for me to sign. You've always been a very smart boy."

"As a matter of fact, I do have a document our attorney drew up."

"Send it to me. I will run it by my lawyer to make sure that, after all is said and done, Alex is still a co-owner."

"I hope that was a joke. I've never given you any reason—"

"Steven, I'm so sorry, so sorry. I'm just too bitter now. So sorry...Send it to me, and I will sign and return it as soon as possible."

"Thanks, Vika. You will have to meet with me to have it notarized. Alex was against of all of this, but he's never had any clue about the legal side of things. He also asked me to tell you that if you decide not to claim the business, you can keep the house. He said that both—the house and the business—were your ideas, anyway. I only wish, Vika, that you would have hired somebody at the time to decide on something other than that stupid company name. Now, even though you are accusing me of being a 'smart boy,' I have also had the attorney draw up a quitclaim for the house, which Alex will sign. Or you can get it from the escrow officer when you are in escrow. You will send it to me and Alex will sign it. Let's make everything as clean and easy as possible."

So the house was mine now. It was very generous of him. In any event, I would not stay there—too painful. Besides, I would never be able to maintain it without Alex. Thus, it remained on the market.

When I was home, Alex stayed at his old friend's place. And then Steven bid out a job in Las Vegas, and Alex and the other four workers moved there temporarily to work on the project, while Steven stayed with the LA office. When this moving and selling business was over, I rented a tiny apartment close to my office. I made decent money on the house. So, in the future, when I would be able to think straight, I could decide whether I wanted to buy my own place or continue renting.

Every two or three months, I would try to pull my head out of my shell and see whether it still hurt to face life. When I saw that it did, I crawled right back inside.

We kept our every-other-Wednesday dinners, Danny and I. I don't know whether it had become a habit to him or was his way of supporting me, but he was maturing, my Danny. I cooked healthy dinners, he brought movies he wanted to watch (partially so that there would be less time spent arguing), and we made it work. I forced myself to be strong and content, and in time, I actually started feeling strong and content—every other Wednesday.

As we were always there for each other, Belka called frequently to offer her unyielding support. I was completely exhausted all the time and was drenched with perspiration after every phone call, so I stopped answering most of them. I saved my energy to go to work and be productive. I could not afford to slip into full-blown depression.

I saw her number pop up on the caller ID; I had to answer at least once every two or three weeks.

"Hi, Vika, how are you?"

"I am just fine, and you, bella mia?"

"I am just fine, too."

"All right, then, good-bye."

"Ha-ha-ha, how funny. You could use some newer jokes. I am so honored that you decided to take my call today. How do you feel? Is your perpetual flu getting any better? I'm telling you, you need to start taking some drugs for your depression."

"I don't have depression. And I cannot stand to hear the word *drugs*."

"You're an idiot! I can't help you if you won't help yourself! I remember when you were in the same condition fifteen-some years ago, just before Alex came along to save you. Oops, that was a bad example. I'm sorry."

"Don't worry, I won't get offended or start fighting with you. I couldn't handle that right now. I have very little left to cling to, so even you count now. But you're wrong. It was different fifteen years ago. I was lost then. And I felt guilty, too. I knew the fact that he was a bad husband made me a bad wife. So we both were losers. And now I am not lost, and I know I was a very good and dedicated wife. I found myself while I was with Alex. I found myself while dealing with Julia. I know who I am now, which helps. I know what I can and cannot do. I know what I want and don't want to be. Common sense, Belka, common sense—it rules. Don't worry about me. I will get through it."

"Did you try to drink? They say it can help."

"Are you just trying to keep the conversation going? You know I can't drink. I never could because it makes me sick. But I sleep. I can sleep all day and all night long. I want to hug my bed and rub it and kiss it and sleep and sleep. And when I cannot sleep anymore, I'm unable to get up, anyway."

"It *is* depression. I don't know what you're waiting for. Do you want me to come?"

"No, I don't want to drive all the way to the airport to get you."

"Want to fly here to visit? It's close to Kathy, too. You could also visit with her. You were very close, if I remember correctly."

"It would be an awkward situation. I don't want her to take sides. It's her brother and her niece, after all. And I'm not even sure if she is on their side, so I definitely don't want to add to Alex's struggle. She tried to call me a few times, but as hard as it was for me to do it, I told her that we couldn't continue any kind of relationship because I refuse to be conspiring with her behind her brother's back."

"You always think of others more than yourself."

"Not anymore. But I am strong. I think Alex will need more support than me."

"And you think *that* is not awkward? Oh well. Whatever. What never changes is your being so very stubborn. I am afraid to ask my next question: How is Danny? How is he taking it?"

"He liked Alex very much, so he is disappointed in me. I put on a brave face when I see him. He hates when I'm weak, so I play the strong woman. But I understand him better now. He has made valid points in any disagreement we've ever had. He is a well-rounded human being in general, and I can be proud of him. Remember how he always called me a people pleaser? I reasoned that it's good for your karma when everybody likes you. His argument was that, in sending the wrong message, you attract all the right and all the wrong people. And what we really need is to have very few right people around us. I could not agree more about that now. Alex taught me that, too. I could never cry on Danny's shoulder, of course, but have you ever found a man with whom you could?"

I could think of one, and I am sure Belka thought of him, too, but this time she was careful to let it pass.

She only said, "I always told you that Danny is a winner— brilliant, handsome, and a big achiever. Good for you as his mother."

"Belka, don't flatter me. It's me, Vika, you're talking to. Don't worry, I'm not suicidal. And how are you, my friend? How is your significant other, and how are your kids?"

"We're fine. They're fine. Enough about me. How is that gestapo friend of yours? What was her name? The shock therapist."

"Maggie. They are very attentive and don't leave me alone. Thank goodness Max fully recuperated after that accident. He's still limping a little, but it's hardly noticeable. Maggie tells him that it makes him look sexier, like a macho man. What a happy lot to sit by your husband's bed, nurture him, and see him get better. Now she has to waste her time with me. I wish everybody would just leave me alone. She is probably jealous of my love affair with my bed."

"Let me know if you want me to come. I need a vacation."

"Thanks, but no thanks. You have plenty to take care of without me. I'll let you know if and when I need you. Listen, I need to go. My bed is calling my name. I am so tired of talking. You talk too much. People talk too much. Thanks for calling."

I hung up, and then I tried to remember whether I asked her how she was. I believed I did.

One particular Wednesday night, Danny came for dinner, and he brought a nice-looking skinny blonde with him. Her name was Angelica, which suited her quite well; she was very lovely and looked like an angel. We had a pleasant time together, eating and joking and all trying to make a good impression on each other. I did my best to speak the most proper English I could master, as I usually did when Danny brought his friends over. I did not want Danny's friends to think his mother was an illiterate immigrant. I was always crazy about any girl Danny would bring over; anybody who could potentially become the mother of my grandchild was a goddess to me. After dinner, Danny took her home and came back to get my opinion, which had never happened before. I don't know whether he never really cared about my input or was just playing it cool, but this time was different. I was always very careful not to upset him, so I would praise her even if I didn't like her—but I did! And that's what I told him. He looked pleased and confirmed how much he liked her, believing that it had the potential to become a serious relationship.

Then he added, "Until recently, she had some drug problems, but now she's in a program and promised it would never happen again. And I believe her."

That stopped me dead in my tracks. I knew I had to pretend I agreed with anything he said, and so I would have under any other circumstances but this. I knew I was inviting a big storm that might aggravate to the point where I would not see him for months, but it was my Danny's life that was at stake, and that was more important than our relationship.

"Danny, remember how I told you once that if you ever come across someone who has drug problems to run for your life? I am telling you now—run. Run while it is not too late, while children are not involved. I would never tell you to do this if she was your wife of many years and this problem occurred. But she is just a new girlfriend. Don't let it develop any further. We could have a dispute and every side would be right and bring all the right arguments. You can disagree with me, and you can hate me, but just listen to me when I say, *don't do it*! As a mother, as an older person, as a person whose life was ruined by drugs, I demand that you stop this relationship right now. I said it to you, and now you can do whatever you think is right, which is what you always do, anyway. But I won't blame myself in the years to come for being a coward not to warn you. Don't make this grave mistake."

"Mother, do you remember our favorite book, *The Little Prince*? 'You become responsible, forever, for what you have tamed'?"

"Then think twice about who to tame. Plus, when it comes to drugs, no rule applies anymore—even that one. And dating somebody for a few weeks doesn't make you responsible for the rest of your life. Just end it at once."

"It was very stupid of me to think that you might understand and support me." He looked at me with an anguished hatred and stormed out of the house. I knew it would take a long time for this ordeal to heal, but I also knew I had no choice.

I tried to assess the damage to my mental state because I was scared that this would be the last straw in my attempt at hanging in there. But I felt nothing new; I was still in the protective coma I had forced upon myself. Plus, it helped knowing I did the only right thing there was to do. Twenty years ago, I would have argued with the person I had become, citing all the powerful arguments: compassion, help, sacrifice, love, and second chances. But now I knew better.

A few more months passed. Greg called me religiously every day at lunchtime; he did not want Nelly to see how much he cared about me. What a solid and dependable person he was. I did not tell him what had happened between Danny and me. I just asked him to call Danny once in a while to check on him. I was not even sure that Danny was in the country.

One Sunday night, Greg called and said that Danny had contacted him earlier that morning and offered to meet them at the beach. Greg and Nelly met him there, and they went out to lunch, where a girl came to join them later. I did not breathe at this point of the story. Greg thought she was a very pretty and very pleasant blonde and liked her a lot, and even Nelly was impressed by how respectful the girl was to her.

I asked if he knew what her name was, and he yelled, "Honey, do you remember the name of Danny's girl?"

Men, they can remember the most random things, except when it comes to what really matters.

Nelly yelled back, "Britta."

Greg said, "Nelly says Britta."

"Greg," I cried, "I love you so much I want to scream. And I adore Nelly! Sometimes she says the most precious words."

"You are becoming really hysterical, and it scares me. Danny said to say hi to you and asked how you were doing."

Now I was crying—no, I was weeping. Go figure. More bad news and I feel nothing; I am numb. But one good or just normal bit of news and I lose it. Hmm, strange. You might be wondering what the good news was. My son said hi to me after disappearing from my life for four months, and I call that good news. But nothing was ever easy in my life, so I learned to appreciate the small things. And considering that I was my grandma's descendant, I decided that I had to be a survivor. My bubbe saved my Danny again. She definitely had connections up there in heaven. She did not save my marriage, but it was a vicious cycle, with no way of breaking it. To get rid of Julia's problems, we had to go through something very horrible, and Alex would not survive it. Not getting rid of Julia's problems meant I had to lose my mind and myself. For Julia to start living a normal life, she had to find brains and values. So all three scenarios were unrealistic, and even my bubbe could offer no help.

That night, Danny called me. He assumed a very casual and nonchalant tone, as if it were only yesterday when he had last called me. I pretended that I hadn't heard anything from

Greg, and he acted as though he believed me. But to go on with life, we had to put something behind us.

"How is it going with Angelica?" I asked.

And he allowed himself one sentence only: "I can put up with plenty, but I cannot take a person lying all the time."

Yep, that's what drugs do. They make you lie constantly. We never mentioned it again. If my very happy, yet very tragic marriage was taken into consideration when Danny was making this decision, it was well worth going through, and I would do it all again in a heartbeat.

M&M became very involved with me again. I was in trouble, and they were there for me, just like the fifteen-some years before Alex. I would lie in bed all weekend again, and they would come over and try to drag me out again. Was I back to square one? No. I knew myself better now, and I liked myself better now. And I regretted nothing. I had a wonderful, wonderful life with Alex—most of the time. A very wonderful man loved me, and it made me a whole woman. I was at peace with myself and was ready to face life again.

EPILOGUE

A little over a year after that memorable Melrose breakfast took place, M&M came over on a Saturday night, and Maggie declared that they were not leaving the house without me. It was their anniversary, and they were going to a fancy new Russian restaurant. After all their continuous support, I could not ignore such an occasion—and I told them that dinner would be my treat. Also, they promised that it would be only the three of us. They planned a big party for the following weekend, but I promptly told them that I would not be attending that one.

I dragged myself to the shower and did my best with my hair (not one of my specialties). I threw on some outfit that fit me better now, because for some reason, I had lost some weight, although it didn't much matter anymore.

They drove me to the restaurant, and we had a very nice dinner—except for the unbearably loud music. If you wanted to say a word to somebody, you had to go outside. But if you went outside, there were people smoking since there are a lot of Russians who smoke, especially women. Maggie went outside for a smoke and gave me a cigarette. *Well, what the heck*, I thought, *I'm not about to start smoking again after one cigarette*. So there we were, standing outside by the restaurant door, when I saw them.

First, I saw a very stunning young woman dressed very daringly, even for a Russian restaurant. It took me a second to recognize Julia, not because she had changed, but because she was so completely out of my life now that my system was not ready to identify her. Then I placed everybody else by association. They were heading straight for the door. It was too late for me to pretend that I didn't see them or for them to turn back, so we had to face each other. It was Julia, Ben, Alex, and some very lovely woman. Julia saw me and let out a scream of joy.

"Victoriaaaaa! Papa, look who's here! How cool to run into you! I miss you! You look nice! You lost some weight. And what a stylish outfit you're wearing tonight! Oh, wait a minute…I remember it. It was in style a few years ago. It actually complements your figure." She ran to me and kissed me, and she kissed Maggie, too. She flooded us with excitement. "What are you doing here? Your anniversary, Maggie? Twenty-five years! My goodness, people don't live that long—just kidding. We are celebrating, too; today is my sixth month of sobriety!"

Six months—so she relapsed again. I looked at Alex, and he looked at me, and I knew that he knew what I was thinking. We still had that unspoken connection between us.

"Papa, say hi to Vika. Vika, you remember Ben, and this is Elena. We dragged my gorgeous dad out on a blind date with Elena tonight."

Poor Alex was evidently in agony. He nodded to us, took his new lady friend under the arm (as he used to do with me at the beginning when we ran into his old acquaintances), and rushed her inside. He had aged so much that I wouldn't have recognized him had I met him on the street. Poor Alex, he always thought it was imperative to look good. But I could tell he never missed his sixty to eighty pushups every morning. Still very lean.

I felt numb. I could not believe I let Maggie talk me into going to a Russian restaurant. I always hated Russian restaurants—and so did Alex. But there was Julia who loved them, and I understood how he ended up being there that night. But me, I had no business being there whatsoever!

Maggie squeezed my hand and said, "This is what you wanted, isn't it? So compose yourself and face it in style."

My dear friend Maggie believed in slapping your face when you are fainting.

We went back inside, and I asked M&M if we could leave. After Max saw Alex, he felt so bad for me that he agreed to leave immediately. But Maggie knowingly said that I had to practice how to act in this situation because Alex and I would undoubtedly run into each other again with the number of mutual friends we had.

"Besides," she said, "you do look nicer than usual, so let them see that you didn't fall apart. Kill them with your looks and laughter!"

"Maggie, I never put on a show. And I don't want to kill him! That is Julia's job. I wish him well. He is a wonderful person."

"You make me sick! If he is such a wonderful person, why have you divorced him? He adored you. It doesn't make any sense."

Lucky Maggie, she had no idea about the rule "drugs in, sense out."

She continued her therapy. "But since you divorced him, you must hate him. It always helps. It will be your victory. Your name is *Victoria*, for God's sake! They just wasted a powerful name on you!"

Max looked so apologetic. "Maggie, you are like a little Stalin, or maybe even a little Hitler. Leave her alone. Let's go dance. It's our anniversary, after all, and we have to start working on our foreplay."

They went to the dance floor, and I decided to drink more wine, knowing full well that it would make me sick in a half hour. I have an intolerance to alcohol. I don't usually drink at all, but if I must drink, I prefer to have a shot of tequila because it has no ramifications afterward. But now all I wanted was to lose myself in anything and stumble into a stupor. As I poured the wine, I caught a glimpse of Alex approaching our table. I quickly gulped down a full glass.

"Hi, Vika. I feel bad that I did not say hi to you. We're certainly not enemies." He stopped, but I could tell he wanted to say something else. "Don't drink, you'll get sick."

"Hi, Alex. Of course we're not enemies."

"You look nice."

Some things never change.

"You look great yourself." It was not true, but unlike him, I didn't care too much about that stuff, about looks and all that. What good did it do him, or even Julia?

"How is Julia?"

Now that she was not my problem anymore, I felt generous. "You know."

"But, Alex, she looks as great as ever." I was smiling, and he smiled, too.

We still had it: We understood each other from the tone of our voice or from just one look.

A moment of uneasy silence followed.

Then he broke it. "All right, then, it was nice seeing you again. I had hoped that when we finally met we wouldn't be enemies. It just caught me off guard."

"Me, too. Don't worry about it. Good luck with Julia. I hope she deserves such sacrifice."

He looked at me very long, and then he turned quickly and left the restaurant.

Oh Alex, my Alex.

∽

ABOUT THE AUTHOR

Rita Kinsky was born in the Soviet Union and immigrated to America in 1989. Although she has gone through both high and low points, many of which are reflected in this book, she always appreciates what this country has to offer hardworking people with strong values. Rita Kinsky lives in Los Angeles with her husband.

Don't miss the dramatic conclusion to Vika's story in the upcoming book by Rita Kinsky. For more information, you can visit ritakinsky.com, follow Rita on Twitter (@RitaKinsky) or contact her at RitaKinsky@yahoo.com.

Made in the USA
Charleston, SC
17 December 2011